FREEWAY

An Integrated Course in Communicative English

STUDENT BOOK 2

Cheryl Pavlik

Anna Stumpfhauser de Hernandez

Contents

1 Questions and Statements with Be, Prepositions of Place

Look at the picture. Complete the conversations.

a. A: ..... dog?
   B: It's ..... tree.
   A: ..... ?
   B: No, ... brown.

b. A: ..... the photographer?
   B: He ..... .
   A: ..... ?
   B: No, ... Canadian.

c. A: ..... the dentist ..... the bank?
   B: No, ...

d. A: ..... the carrots ..... the chair?
   B: Yes, ...

e. A: ..... the apples?
   B: ..... on ..... , ... the supermarket.

2 Simple Present Tense

1. Fill in the blanks.

Hi! My name's Jessica Morton. I'm [1] ..... Ireland, but I [2] ..... in Seattle, Washington. I'm a computer programmer and I [3] ..... for Kimball Industries. I have a lot of friends but I don't have a boyfriend right now. I [4] ..... sports a lot. In the evenings, I [5] ..... bowling, or I [6] ..... tennis. On weekends, my friends and I like to [7] ..... in the lake near Seattle.

2. Now write a letter home. Tell your mother about your new friend, Jessica Morton. Begin like this.

Dear Mom,
I have a new friend. Her name is Jessica Morton. She...

3 Directions

Listen and match the places below to the map.

the park   the swimming pool   the Manitou Movie Theater
the Western Hills Hotel   the library

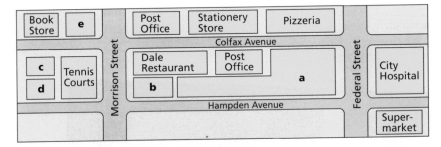

4 Questions with Be, Do and Can

1. You are looking for a job. Write questions to complete
this job application form.

1. Name..
2. Address..
....
3. Telephone number...
4. Age...................
5. Nationality..
6. Married/divorced/single.................................
7. Children.......................

8. Occupation...
9. Abilities
   a. play an instrument
   b. speak a language
   c. sports
10. Leisure time activities...
....
....

2. Now ask your partner your questions and fill in his/her
answers. Then report to the class.

5 Family Relationships, Possessives

Look at the family tree. Complete the sentences.
Cate is Bob's [1] ..... . Cate and Bob have two [2] ..... , Kevin and
Justin, and one [3] ..... , Michelle. Kevin and Justin are [4].....
brothers. Justin is [5] ..... husband and [6] ..... [7] ..... name is Robert.
Cate is [8] ..... grandmother and Bob is [9] ..... grandfather. Michelle
is Robert's [10] ..... .

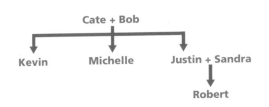

6 Find the Errors

Find the errors in the sentences. Then correct them.
a. This are my pens.
b. What time you have English class?
c. Would you like a rice?
d. Victor can plays the guitar.
e. I not like to play cards.
f. Erika is from Brazilian.

At the Start

How old are the people in the pictures?
Read the interviews in *Health Magazine* and find out.

Maggie Perkins is 108 years old and lives in Centerville, Indiana.

MAGGIE: The secret of my life? That's easy, D-W-A-S-T.

REPORTER: DWAST?

MAGGIE: It means "don't worry about small things." I'm always healthy because I never worry and I rarely get angry.

REPORTER: Do you get tired or bored?

MAGGIE: Tired?! Of course I get tired. I'm 108 years old! But bored, never!

REPORTER: Why not, Maggie?

MAGGIE: Because I really enjoy new things, like those music videos the kids watch these days. They're really exciting.

Bob Moore is 102 years old and lives in Vancouver, British Columbia.

REPORTER: Can you tell us the secret of your long life, Mr. Moore?

BOB: Yes, I can Kevin. It's broccoli! I eat it everyday. Great stuff, broccoli.

REPORTER: Broccoli? Are you a vegetarian?

BOB: Almost. I rarely eat meat.

REPORTER: And do you exercise?

BOB: Oh yes. I'm usually careful about that.

REPORTER: Do you exercise every day?

BOB: Yep. I ride my bicycle every day.

REPORTER: Your bicycle? Oh, you mean an exercise bicycle in your house.

BOB: Of course not! Every day I ride my bicycle to the park and play basketball with the boys!

REPORTER: The boys?

BOB: Sure. There's a group of men who play basketball in the park. I call them the boys because they're only in their sixties and seventies.

Read the interviews above again and answer the questions.
a. Does Maggie get tired?
b. What does DWAST mean?
c. What vegetable does Bob eat every day?
d. Who plays basketball everyday?

1 Spotlight

1. Study the adverbs of frequency below.

I *always* worry.	I am *always* lazy.
You *usually* worry.	You are *usually* lazy.
He *often* worries.	He is *often* lazy.
She *never* worries.	He is *never* lazy.
We *rarely* worry.	We are *rarely* lazy.
They *sometimes* worry.	They are *sometimes* lazy.

always → 100

usually →

often →

50

sometimes →

rarely →

never → 0

2. Complete these sentences with *before* and *after*.

a. With the verb *be* the adverbs of frequency are ..... the verb.

b. With verbs other than *be*, the adverbs of frequency are ..... the verb.

3. Rearrange the words to make correct sentences.

a. meat eat usually for I lunch.   b. angry is in often class Bill.

2 Words to Remember

1. Study the words below.

get angry   get tired   get bored

2. Complete these sentences.

a. I always get bored when ..... .   b. I usually get angry when ..... .   c. I never get tired when ..... .

3 Listening

Listen to Chris and Sam talk about themselves. Complete the table with the adverbs of frequency.

	get up early	worry	exercise	go to bed early	get bored	get angry
Chris						
Sam						

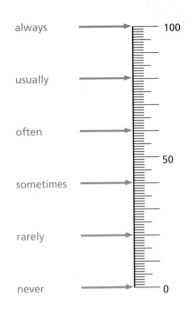

4 Practice

Look at the table in *Listening* above. Make sentences about Chris and Sam.

5 Talk in Pairs and Groups

Complete the table in *Listening* above for yourself and your partner. Write your partner's answers. Then tell the class about your partner.

6 Writing

Write about the daily activities of someone that you know.

At the Start WF

1. Look at these pictures. Do you know the names of any of the animals? Answer the questions. Look at page 79 for the answers.

a. Some of these animals are dangerous. Which ones are they?

b. Some people eat one of the animals here. Which one is it?

c. Do any of these animals have any unusual habits?

d. There aren't any ..... in Ireland or Hawaii.

a.

b.

d.

e.

c.

1 Words to Remember WF

1. Look in the Wordfinder. Find:
three unusual pets
two dangerous animals
three poisonous animals
a large animal
two animals that people eat

2. Make a sentence with six of the words in the Wordfinder.
Example:
I don't like spiders.

2 Spotlight

1. Look at the structures.

> Are there *any* snakes in Hawaii?
>   No, there aren't *any* snakes but there are *some* lizards.
> Do *some* people like unusual pets?
>   Yes, *some* people do.

2. Look at the sentences above. Check the correct column.

	Questions	Affirmative statements	Negative statements
Use *some* in			
Use *any* in			

> **!** Both *some* and *any* are used in questions. We usually use *some* in offers or when we expect the answer to be yes.
> Example:
> *Would you like **some** coffee/help?*
> *Do we have **any** peanut oil?*

3 Practice

Complete the conversation with *some, any* or *a*.

A: Excuse me, do you have [1] ..... canaries?
B: No, I'm sorry. We don't have [2] ..... canaries right now. But we have [3] ..... other birds.
A: What kind of birds do you have?
B: Well, let's see. We have [4] ..... doves and [5] ..... parrots.
A: Can the parrots talk?
B: Well, [6] ..... parrots can talk.
A: What language do they speak?
B: You have to teach them to speak your language.
A: I'm not [7] ..... very good teacher. Don't you have [8] ..... parrots that have already finished language school?
B: Sorry sir. We have [9] ..... parrots but they are all uneducated.

4 Listening

1. 🔲 Listen to this conversation in a stationery store. Write the four things that the woman asks for.

2. 🔲 Listen again. Which of these items does the store have?

3. 🔲 Listen again. What is the woman's problem at the end?

5 Role Play

Student A: You need some unusual kinds of food. Ask the clerk for these things:

bean sprouts

mangoes

fish sauce

rice from Thailand

coconut milk

Student B: You are a clerk in a grocery store. Answer Student A's questions. You have some items but you don't have everything.

6 Writing

You are in another country. Write a letter to your best friend. Ask him/her to send you some things that you cannot find. Begin like this:

> Dear *Pablo*,
> How are you? Everything is fine here in *San Francisco*.
> My only problem is that I can't find...

At the Start

Look at the pictures. Where are the men? Are they waiting for someone?

1 Listening

1.  Read the questions. Then listen and answer them.

a. Who is Steve talking about?
  1. his sister   **2.** his girlfriend
  3. his neighbor
b. What is her name?
  1. Darlene   **2.** Debbie   **3.** Dianne
c. Why are the men surprised?

2. 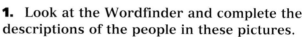 Listen to the tape again and choose the picture of the woman.

a.

b.

c.

d.

2 Words to Remember

1. Look at the Wordfinder and complete the descriptions of the people in these pictures.

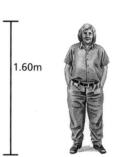

1.60m

1.80m

a. short and .....   **c.** ..... gray hair
b. long ..... hair   **d.** ..... and thin

2. Put the adjectives in the previous activity in the correct columns below.

HAIR		
length	type	color
short	straight	brown

EYES	
size	color
small	

BODY TYPE	
height	weight
tall	thin

3 Spotlight

1. Study the structure below.

Order of descriptive adjectives:

length/type/color hair
short curly blond hair

size/color eyes
big brown eyes

brunette

2. Put these noun phrases in order.
a. small eyes blue
b. black long hair straight

4 Talk in Pairs WF

Tell your partner about a friend.
Example:
My best friend's name is Miguel. He's short and thin. He has short black hair.

5 Writing

Write about your partner's best friend. Tell your partner to check your description.

6 Reading

1. Read the article below. Then choose the best title.
a. How to be a Successful Model
b. Modeling is a Beautiful Business
c. Not All Models are Beautiful ✓
d. Famous Models

2. The article mentions seven different types of models. Can you find them all?

3. The word *model* is used in two different ways. Write the sentences which show these two ways in your notebook. Which sentence uses *model* as a noun? Which uses *model* as a verb?

Do you think all models are tall, thin and beautiful? If you said yes, you're wrong. There are many models who are not beautiful at all. Some are hand models or foot models. Others are nose models, hair models or back models. These people model the hands in a watch advertisement or the feet in a shoe advertisement. Sometimes they work with famous models who have beautiful faces but ugly hands or feet.

There are also other kinds of specialized modeling. Funnyface Agency in New York employs "ordinary" people for certain kinds of advertising. For example, a famous model might look foolish washing dishes or eating cereal. For these kind of advertisements photographers want people who look "normal."

Plus Models agency in New York looks for women who are tall and large to model clothes for large-size women. Susan Georget,

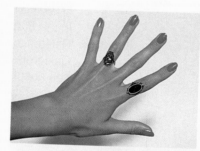

an executive for Plus Models says, "Top large-size models can work every day and make more than one hundred thousand dollars a year."

Modeling is still a very difficult business but you don't have to be young, thin and gorgeous to be successful.

very beautiful

fowl – birds that we eat
foul – an action that is against the rules a game

At the Start

1. Can you bowl? What do you think turkey bowling is?
Read the article and find out.

Would you like to try turkey bowling?

How do you turkey-bowl?

First you put ten large plastic bottles of soft drinks on the floor. Then you throw a frozen turkey across the floor and try to knock down the bottles.

Of course, turkey bowling has rules just like other sports. You don't have to wear a uniform, but:

1. You have to stand behind the fowl* line. You can't put your foot across this line.
2. You have to slide the turkey across the floor. You can't throw it.
3. You have to use a frozen turkey. You can't use a chicken but you can choose a big turkey or a small one.
4. You have to take the turkeys home and eat them.

Where can you go turkey bowling?

In the Santa Ana food market in Santa Ana, California. It's becoming a popular sport in California and the Turkey Bowlers' Association has about 2,000 members. Of course you have to go at night. You can't turkey bowl when there are people in the store.

* fowl= a bird that people eat
foul= an action that is against the rules of a game

2. Look at the picture. Find the three rules that he's breaking.

1 Spotlight

1. Study the structures below.

Do you **have to** use a turkey?	Yes, you do.
Do you **have to** use a big turkey?	No, you don't
You **have to** stand behind the foul line.	
You **don't have to** wear a uniform.	

2. Make a list of things that students in your school *have to* and *don't have to* do.

2 Listening WF

🔊 Listen to information about another sport. Check what you *have to* and *don't have to* do, and what you *can* and *can't* do. Then guess what the sport is.

	have to	don't have to	can	can't
hit the ball over the net	✓		✓	
use a racket	✓			✓
hit the ball with your hand				✓
always stand behind the line		✓		
move around the court			✓	
move fast	✓			
jump over the net	✓	✓		✓

You

3 Practice WF

1. Look at the table in *Listening* and make sentences with *have to, don't have to* and *can/can't*.

2. Now make similar sentences about a sport that you know. Tell your partner about it.

4 Talk in Pairs

1. Tell your partner about your responsibilities at home, school or work. What things do you have to do?
Example:

> I have to cook breakfast every day.

2. Tell your class about things that your partner has to do but you don't have to do.
Example:

> Manuel has to wash the dishes every day but I don't have to.

5 Writing

Write about your responsibilities using *have to* and *don't have to*.

6 Pronunciation

1. 🔊 Listen. Which word do you hear?
a. wait   gate
b. one   gun
c. Wes   guess
d. will   gill
e. would   good
f. way   gay
g. west   guest
h. whirl   girl

2. 🔊 Listen and repeat the sentences.
Would you please wait at the gate?
One girl will go west with Wanda.
Where will we find the wood?

1 Words to Remember `WF`

1. Match the names with the parts of the
body. Check your answers in the
Wordfinder.

arm   back   foot   hand   head
leg   neck   stomach throat   tooth

> **!** one tooth/two teeth
> **•** one foot/two feet

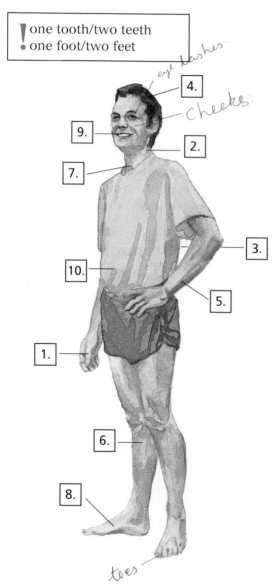

eye lashes

cheeks

4.

9.

2.

7.

3.

10.

5.

1.

6.

8.

toes

2. Describe a monster to your partner.
He/She will draw it.
Example:
It has two heads and eight arms. It ...

2 Listening

1. 📟 Listen and number the people.

a.

b.

c.

d.

e.

f.

2. 📟 Listen to the conversations again.
Find a different way to say these things.
a. I have a headache.
b. She has a stomachache.
c. His tooth hurts.
d. My back hurts.

3. 📟 Listen to another conversation
between a doctor and a patient and answer
the questions.
a. What is the patient's problem?
b. What is the doctor's suggestion?

teeth — 32

3 Role Play

1. Match each health problem with its remedy.

1. a fever   a. Take aspirin.
2. a sore throat   b. Take vitamin C.
3. a cold   c. Have only tea and toast for 24 hours.
4. a backache   d. Take aspirin and drink a lot of water.
5. a stomachache   e. Drink tea with honey and lemon.
6. a headache   f. Sleep on a hard bed.

2. Student A: You are the patient.
Student B: You are the doctor.
Have a conversation. Then change roles.

Doctor   Patient

What's the problem?

I have .....

Do you have a .....

Yes, and .....

Take .....

Okay. Thank you.

4 Reading

1. Read the article below. Then answer *true* or *false*.

a. Some people think hot onions are good for colds. T
b. Cold germs can only live inside your body. F
c. Scientists believe that chicken soup helps colds. T
d. People don't buy medicine for colds because it doesn't help. F

2. Check the symptoms of a cold.

a. A runny nose.
b. A stomachache.
c. A fever.
d. A sore throat.
e. A toothache.

5 Talk in Groups

Tell your class about some home remedies.

6 Writing

Write about some home remedies.

The Cold Facts

Do you have a scratchy throat?
Does your nose run?
Do you have trouble sleeping?
Do you feel generally miserable?

If your answer is yes, you probably have the common cold.

Some Cold Facts
◆ Sixty percent (60%) of all health problems are colds.
◆ In the United States people with colds miss 30 million days of school and work every year.
◆ People in the United States spend $3 billion a year on cold remedies.
◆ Cold germs can live three hours on your hands and clothes.

Cold Wives Tales
Here are some unusual remedies. Believe it or not, people use them!
◆ Put a fish skin on your feet.
◆ Put a piece of carrot in your nose.
◆ Put hot fried onions on your chest.

Home Remedies that Work
◆ Chicken soup. (No one knows why, but research shows that it makes you feel better.)
◆ Hot water with lemon juice.
◆ Oranges and lemons cooked with honey and lemon juice.

At the Start

Look at the picture.
What is it?

What was it?

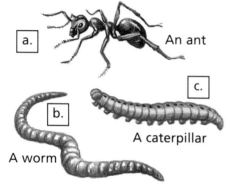

a.

b.

c.

An ant

A caterpillar

A worm

1 Spotlight

1. Study the structures below.

What ***was*** Sputnik?
It ***was*** the first spacecraft.

Who ***were*** the Supremes?
They ***were*** a singing group.

Who ***was*** Rudolph Valentino?
He ***was*** an actor.

Where ***were*** you yesterday?
I ***was*** at home.

2. Look at the structures above. Complete the sentences.
a. I ..... at the party. was
b. You ..... sick. were
c. She ..... at work. was

TRIVIA

How many of these trivia questions can you answer?

1. Where were potatoes from originally? Preu
2. Who was Rudolph Valentino?
3. Who were the Supremes?
4. Who was the first man on the moon? Neil Armstorng
5. What was Sputnik? 1957 mand made Satilitte USSR
6. How many dwarfs were with Snow White?
7. Who was Gandhi?
8. What were the Niña, the Pinta and the Santa Maria? ships
9. How many Star Wars movies were there? 3
10. Where was Babylon? Irak

2 Listening

 Listen to Jill and Joe have an argument. Then answer the questions.

a. The party was for
   1. graduation.   2. New Year's.   3. someone's birthday.
b. Joe was at the party with
   1. Jill.   2. Penny.   3. Patty.
c. Jill was at the party with
   1. Jerry.   2. Tom.   3. Joe.
d. All the girls were in love with
   1. Joe.   2. Jerry.   3. Tom.

3 Practice

1. Complete the paragraph with these words: *was, wasn't, were, weren't.*

Jill and Joe's argument ¹was about a party. The party ²was at Jill's house. It ³was a New Year's party. About fifty people ⁴were there. Joe ⁵was at the party too but Jill and Joe ⁶were at the party together. Joe ⁷was there with Penny Morton. Jill ⁸was there with Jerry Thompson. Jill thinks that Jerry ⁹was very good-looking. Joe thinks that he ¹⁰wasn't.

2. Use the cues to make questions about the party and ask your partner.

a. Where/party?
b. When/party?
c. How many people/there?
d. Joe and Jill together?
e. Who/there with Joe?
f. Who/there with Jill?

4 Talk in Pairs WF

Ask about your partner's first friend, toys, house, and teacher.
Example:

What was your first toy?

It was a beautiful doll with long brown hair.

5 Writing WF

Write a paragraph about one of the people or places in *Talk in Pairs.* Include as much detail as you can remember.

6 Pronunciation

 Listen to the five sentences. Do you hear *where* or *were*? Then listen again and repeat.

At the Start

1. Read the article about Gordon Sumner.
Can you guess his other name?

sting

Gordon Sumner

Who is he?

a. From 1972 to 1974, he taught elementary school.

b. In 1989, he wrote a book called Jungle Stories about the problems in the Amazon rain forest.

c. He was born in Newcastle, England in 1951.

d. Today he continues singing and working to help the people in the Amazon rain forest.

e. He joined The Police as lead singer in 1977.

f. In 1985, he began his solo career.

g. He went to a meeting about problems in the rain forests of the world in 1990.

h. He sang at Nelson Mandela's 70th birthday party in June 1988.

i. In September 1988, he toured 17 cities.

2. Put the events in order.

3. Find the verbs in each sentence.

4. Find one verb in the present tense.

5. All the other verbs are in the ..... tense.

1 Words to Remember

Find the past tense of these verbs in the information about Gordon Sumner.

Regular	
present	**past**
tour	toured
join	joined
work	worked
live	lived
study	studied

Irregular	
present	**past**
teach	taught
go	went
write	wrote
sing	sang
begin	began
have	had

2 Spotlight

1. Study the structures below.

I You He/she/it We They	*worked* *went*	hard yesterday. to school last week.

| ! carry ➡ carr*ied* |
| • study ➡ stud*ied* |

2. Write the past tense of these regular verbs.
need   marry   change

3. Look in the irregular verb list on page 80. Find the past tense of these irregular verbs.
win   come   make

_ed_

Diana Ross

3 Practice

1. Write the verbs in the correct form of the past tense.

a. She began to sing with _the Supremes_ in the 19.5.0.
   _{begin}

b. She made her first movie in 19.1.2. It was called _Lady Sings the Blues._
   _{make}

c. In 19.6.7. the group changed its name to _Diana Ross and the Supremes._
   _{change}

d. She was born in Detroit in ..1.9.4 4
   _{be}

e. Her second movie was called _Mahogany._ It came out in 19.7.5.
   _{be} ... _{come}

f. The Supremes worked hard and after a few years they became big stars.
   _{work} ... _{become}

g. Then Diana Ross ..... to start making movies.
   _{decide}
   decided

2. [cassette] Now listen to the information about Diana Ross and fill in the dates.

3. Put the events in number 1 in order.

4. Look at the timeline. Talk about the life of Grace Kelly in the past tense.

1929	1951	1954	1956	1957	1982
is born	goes to Hollywood and makes her first film	wins Academy Award	marries Prince Ranier of Monaco	has her first child, Caroline	dies

4 Talk in Pairs

Make a timeline for yourself until one year ago.
Tell your partner about your life.

5 Writing

Write a paragraph about your partner's life.

6 Pronunciation

1. [cassette] Listen to the three kinds of regular past tense verb endings.

/t/	/d/	/id/
looked	cleaned	needed
washed	described	wanted

2. [cassette] Now listen and put each verb in the correct column above.
dried dusted fixed greeted kicked learned played studied talked
visited walked watched

3. [cassette] Listen and repeat these sentences.
a. We watched while the children played.
b. I studied and they talked.
c. She washed and dried the dishes.
d. They dusted and cleaned.

Review 1: Units 1–7

1. **Find the errors in the sentences. Then correct them.**

a. We don't have some pets in our house.

b. My girlfriend has long yellow hair.

c. I have bad cold.

d. Where were your brother last night?

e. How often Margy goes to the movies?

f. He has tall and thin with black hair.

g. We was at the disco.

h. They can't to play very well.

2. **Fill the spaces with the correct form of the verb.**

A: You weren't at the party last night, Jane. Where ^{1} ..... you?
  _{be}

B: Well, I ^{2} ..... a problem. When I ^{3} ..... in my
  _{have} _{get}
  car I ^{4} ..... that I ^{5} ..... a flat tire. I ^{6} ..... Susie
  _{see} _{have} _{call}
  but she ^{7} ..... at home so I ^{8} ..... home and
  _{not/be} _{stay}
  ^{9} ..... a book.
  _{read}

A: And what about your flat tire?

B: Well, my neighbor ^{10} ..... it for me this
  _{change}
  morning.

A: That's pretty sexist! A man ^{11} ..... change
  _{have to}
  your tire!

B: A man? My neighbor ^{12} ..... a woman.
  _{be}
  She ^{13} ..... great with cars! And she always
  _{be}
  ^{14} ..... what to do.
  _{know}

3. **Unscramble these sentences and questions. Use capital letters where necessary.**

a. always/Mr./the/on/Cohen/works/weekends/.

b. Ireland/are/snakes/any/in/there/?

c. sore/I/a/throat/have/.

d. have/work/she/to/doesn't/ tomorrow/.

e. the/you/how/do/car/often/wash/?

f. now/have/to/the/wash/we/dishes/don't/.

4. **Write questions.**

a. ..... ? Sure, I can.

b. ..... ? No, he doesn't have to.

c. ..... ? Yes, there are some.

d. ..... ? They were at the bank.

e. ..... ? No, she didn't.

f. ..... ? Yes, I do.

5. **Write descriptions of these people.**

6. 📼 Read the statements. Then listen to the radio commercial and complete them.

a. Vitamin Cure is a kind of ..... .

b. Take Vitamin Cure when you have a ..... .

c. Vitamin Cure ..... expensive.

d. You can buy Vitamin Cure at Wonder .... Avenue and ..... Street.

7. Continue logically with another sentence.

a. A: Were you a good student in primary school?

   B: ..... .

b. A: I have a headache.

   B: ..... .

c. A: I have to do a lot of things today.

   B: ..... ?

d. A: I'm sorry. Janet isn't here.

   B: ..... ?

e. A: We have a new teacher.

   B: ..... ?

f. A: I wrote a letter yesterday.

   B: ..... ?

8. Look at the verbs below and choose the correct past tense pronunciation: /t/, /d/, or /id/.

a. washed   b. remembered   c. wanted   d. worked   e. needed   f. liked   g. loved

9. Use the words and phrases to make sentences. Be careful! Sometimes you have to change the form of the verb. Not all combinations are correct.

My mother	sometimes		is		study	to the doctor.
		doesn't	have to		exercise	history class.
The students					worry	about money.
					short	a uniform.
His car	always		was		eat	here.
					expensive	medicine.
		didn't	are	not	go to	yesterday.
					wear	aspirin.
People			were		stay	home.
	never				intelligent	good food.
Sam			am		take	the hospital.
					run	at the store.
I		don't	has to		beautiful	every day.
					have	
			be			

phrase – no subject no verb

At the Start

1. 🔲 Listen to the beginning of the conversation, look at the pictures, and put the phrases in order.

a. Next week. *E*

b. Next week? *F*

c. Hello, can I speak to Carol, please? *D*

d. This is Tim. When will she be back? *A*

e. Hello. *A*

f. I'm sorry. She isn't here right now. Who's calling please? *C*

2. 🔲 Listen to the rest of the conversation and answer the questions.

a. What is Tim's problem?

b. Where does Tim's friend Carol work?

1 Words and Phrases to Remember

1. Study the words and phrases below.

> Hello.

> Can I speak to *Doris*?

> Just a minute.

> Who's calling please?

> This is *Tom*.

> Would you like to leave a message?

> Can I leave a message?

> Please ask *her* to call *me*.

> When will *she* be back?

> She'll be back about *four o'clock*.

> I'll call back later.

> Sorry, (you have the) wrong number.

2. Choose a phrase from the list to complete each exchange.

a. A: Can I speak to Phil?
   B: ...*sorry you have the wrong number?*
   A: Oh, I'm sorry.

b. A: *would you like to leave a message?*
   B: Yes, would you ask him to call Beth?

c. A: Can I speak to George?
   B: ...*Just a minute*
   C: Hello. This is George.

d. A: .....? *Can I speak to Martha?*
   B: I'm sorry. She isn't here right now.
   A: .....? *Can I leave a message?*
   B: Sure. Let me get a pencil and paper.

e. A: I'm sorry. Martha isn't here right now.
   B: That's okay. ....*I'll call back later*

(One moment please
Hold on
wait. Just a minute, please)

22

2 Spotlight

1. Study the structures below.

Subject	Object
I	Please call *me*.
you	I'll call *you*.
he, she	Ask *him* to call *her*.
it	Buy *it* tomorrow.
they, we	Tell *them* to call *us*.

2. Complete the sentences by changing the names to object pronouns.

a. Tell ..... to call ..... .
<small>Paul</small>   <small>Tom and I</small>

b. Would you like to leave a message for ..... ?
<small>Carol</small>

c. Please give ..... this message from ..... .
<small>Sandra</small>   <small>I</small>

d. Ask ..... to write to ..... .
<small>John</small>   <small>Paula's parents</small>

e. Tell ..... he can call ..... tomorrow.
<small>Fred</small>   <small>Bill and Sam</small>

3 Role Play

With a partner, practice making phone calls and answering the telephone.

4 Reading

1. Quickly read the article and choose the best title:

a. The History of *Hello*
b. A Very Important Word
c. Thomas Alva Edison and the Telephone
d. *Hello* in Different Languages

2. Answer *true, false* or *I don't know*.

a. *Hello* is a very old word.
b. *Hello* is a very common word today.
c. Thomas Alva Edison invented the telephone.
d. The word "hello" probably comes from "halloo."
e. All countries use the word "hello" when they answer the telephone.

3. What do people say when they answer the telephone in your country?

The word "hello" is so common that it's difficult to believe that it's only about 100 years old. It's a very small word, but it says many things. It says, "Here I am;" it asks "Are you ready to talk?"; it says "Let's communicate."

Alexander Graham Bell

Allen Koenigsberg, a teacher at Brooklyn College, investigated the origin of "hello." After Alexander Graham Bell invented the telephone, people did not know how to start a conversation when they picked up the phone.

Alexander Graham Bell started using the word "ahoy" to show he was ready to talk. However, when another inventor, Thomas Alva Edison, invented the phonograph in 1877, he shouted "halloo!" into the mouthpiece. "Halloo" was a British word that hunters used. Possibly, he liked the sound of the word and so he continued to use it. Eventually, more and more people used Edison's "hello" rather than Bell's "ahoy."

Today "hello" is used in many different countries. However, some countries use other words or phrases. For example, the Japanese say

"moshi moshi" to mean that someone wants to talk on the telephone. And in Colombia people often say, "a la orden" when they answer the telephone. This means, "at your service."

Thomas Alva Edison

At the Start

Look at the cartoon and answer the questions.

a. Where are these men?
   1. At school.   **2.** At work.   **3.** In the army.
b. Are they good soldiers?
   1. Probably yes.   **2.** Probably no.

1 Words to Remember   WF

1. Make phrases with the verbs and nouns.
Example:
wash your clothes

Verbs
clean   water   iron   make   cut   put away sweep   take out   vacuum   wash

Nouns
the garbage   your clothes   the carpet the floor   the dishes   your bed   the grass the plants   your room

2. Now make sentences with the phrases. Tell your partner how often you do these things.
Example:
I never sweep the floor.

2 Spotlight

1. Study the structures below.

Did	I you he/she we they	*vacuum?*

Yes	I you he/she	*did.*
No	we they	*didn't.*

2. Look at the boxes and correct each sentence.

a. Did you cleaned the floor?
b. Did he washing the dishes?
c. Does she vacuumed her room?

3 Practice `WF`

1. 🔊 Listen and use the words under each cartoon to write the questions you hear.

a. lunch?

c. chili/too hot?

b. apologize?

d. your room?

2. Write five questions to ask your partner about the housework that they did yesterday. Then ask your partner the questions.

Example:

(Did you wash the dishes?)   (No, I didn't.)

4 Pronunciation

🔊 Listen and choose the sentence you hear. Then listen again and repeat.

a. You go to school.
Did you go to school?

b. You wash the floors.
Did you wash the floors?

c. You clean your room.
Did you clean your room?

d. You make dinner.
Did you make dinner?

5 Talk in Groups `WF`

Look at the phrases below. Find someone who/whose...

a. washed their car last night.
b. went shopping yesterday.
c. father bought a car last year.
d. family went on vacation last summer.
e. took out the garbage this morning.
f. watched the news on TV this morning.

At the Start

1. Look at the pictures. Which person is apologizing?

2. Read these apologies and match them with the pictures.
1. "I'm sorry, I forgot your newspaper. I'll bring it later."
2. "I'm very sorry. I broke your glass. I'll buy you another one."
3. "Sorry I'm late. I'll come on time tomorrow."
4. "I'm sorry I didn't do my homework. I promise I'll do it tonight."
5. "I'm very sorry I tore your picture. I'll fix it for you."
6. "Oh no! I left your book at home."

3. Match the responses to the apologies in 2.
a. "That's all right. I'll get one this afternoon."
b. "Yes, please. It's my favorite picture."
c. "That's okay, but you have to bring it to class tomorrow."
d. "Don't buy a new one. I have lots of glasses."
e. "Don't worry. Everyone was late."
f. "My French book? I really need it today."

4. 🖭 Now listen and see if you were correct.

1 Words to Remember

1. Look at the conversations again and complete the table with the missing verbs.

Present	Past	Present	Past
.....	bought	break	.....
.....	brought	forget	.....
.....	came	leave	.....
.....	got	tear	.....
.....	did		

2. Complete the sentences with the correct form of the verbs above.

a. Oh no! I ..... the paper.
b. Mark ..... his wallet in the car.
c. She ..... her skirt on the old chair.
d. He ..... to the party late.
e. Look! I ..... a book for you at the new bookstore.
f. He ..... my new watch and I'm very angry.

2 Spotlight

1. Study the promises with *will*.

I **will** return your money tomorrow.
He**'ll** be here at ten.
We **will** not leave without you.
They **won't** go before tomorrow.

2. Look at the box and complete these sentences.

a. The contraction of *will* is ..... .
b. The contraction of *will not* is ..... .

3 Listening

Listen to the conversations. Complete the sentences.
a. He ..... late again.
b. She ..... the book tomorrow.
c. He ..... the money next week.
d. He ..... another clock.
e. She ..... her homework tomorrow.

4 Practice

Make a promise for each situation.
a. You broke one of your mother's best cups.
b. You left your brother's jacket at a party.
c. You don't have the money that you owe your friend.
d. You forgot to buy bread for your mother.
e. You had an accident in your father's car.

5 Reading

1. Listen to the song and read the words. Then answer the questions.
a. Who is singing the song?
b. Who are they singing to?

2. Find three promises in the song.

3. Read the definitions and find the words.
a. very small
b. give someone a part of what you have
c. hold on to
d. feel sad

For Baby For Bobby

I'll walk in the rain by your side,
I'll cling to the warmth of your tiny hand,
I'll do anything to help you understand,
I'll love you more than anybody can.

And the wind will whisper your name to me,
Little birds will sing along in time,
The leaves will bow down when you walk by,
And morning bells will chime.

I'll be there when you're feeling down,
To kiss away the tears if you cry,
I'll share with you, all the happiness I've found,
A reflection of the love in your eyes.

At the Start

1. Look at the story. Find the names of these people:

the detective   the victim   the wife
the doctor   the butler   the niece

2. Read the story. Can you guess who the killer is? Look on page 79 for the answer.

One night Sherlock Holmes got a telephone call from his friend, Dr. Watson. "Someone murdered David Casters!" he said. "Please come quickly!"

Holmes went to David Casters' home. There at the desk was the body of the dead man. There was a gun on the desk. "This gun is the murder weapon," said Dr. Watson. "But the murderer didn't shoot him. He hit him on the head. David called me yesterday and invited me to dinner. He said that he wanted to talk to me about something. When I got here, he was dead."

"There were only three people home. David's niece, Isabel, his butler, Graves, and his wife, Caroline," said Watson. "I want to talk to all of them," Holmes said.

"I worked for Mr. Casters for thirty years. He was a good employer. I didn't shoot him," said Graves. "What happened tonight?" Holmes asked. "Dr. Watson arrived about seven, but when I went to the library to call Mr. Casters he was already dead," Graves said. "Did you touch the gun?" asked Holmes. "No I didn't. I left it on the desk," answered Graves.

"I'm sorry Mrs. Casters but I must talk to you," said Holmes. "I just can't believe it! David dead! We only had two short wonderful years together!" exclaimed Caroline Casters. "Whose gun is this?" asked Holmes. "I don't know. I didn't know that David had a gun and I don't know who shot him," cried Mrs. Casters.

"Oh I'm very upset, Mr. Holmes. Uncle David was always so kind to me," said Isabel. "Did you touch this gun?" asked Holmes. "No I didn't. I didn't hit him with it either. I didn't even go into the library!"

"Did you tell anyone how he died?" Holmes asked Watson. "I told you but I didn't tell anyone else," said Watson.

"Well, I know who the killer is," said Holmes to Watson.

1 Words to Remember

1. Look at the story. Find verbs in the story to complete the table:

Present	Past
get	. . .
hit	. . .
. . .	knew
. . .	shot
tell	. . .

2. Complete the sentences with the past tense of the verbs above.

a. Dr. Watson ..... Sherlock Holmes about the murder.

b. No one ..... David Casters.

c. The murderer ..... him with the gun.

d. At the end Holmes ..... the name of the murderer.

e. Dr. Watson ..... a telephone call from David Casters.

2 Spotlight

1. Study the structures below.

I You He She We They	*killed* *didn't kill*	him.

2. How many negative verbs in the past tense can you find in the story?

3 Practice

Complete the paragraph with the correct form of the past tense.

"Well, Watson. This is a very interesting case. At first I ^{1}..... (not/know) who the murderer was, but now I do."

"Tell me, Holmes, who ^{2}..... (be) it?"

"It's really very easy to see. The most important thing is that the murderer ^{3}..... (use) a gun, but he or she ^{4}..... (not/shoot) him. The murderer ^{5}..... (hit) him. Now, I ^{6}..... (not/tell) them that. Did you?"

"No, I ^{7}..... (not/tell) them either."

"Well, first there was the butler. Really he ^{8}..... (not/have) a reason to kill Mr. Casters. Then there was the wife and the niece. The wife ^{9}..... (not/know) that the killer ^{10}..... (hit) her husband with the gun. But the niece ^{11}..... (know). She said, 'I ^{12}..... (not/hit) him.' Now, only you and I and the murderer ^{13}..... (know) that."

4 Listening

🔊 Listen to the conversation. Make a list of the things that Nancy didn't do.

5 Talk in Pairs

1. Make a list of five things that you didn't do yesterday. Tell your partner.

2. Report the three most interesting things that your partner didn't do.

6 Writing   WF

Write a letter apologizing for something that you didn't do and give a reason. Begin like this:

Dear Mary,
I'm sorry that I didn't..

At the Start

1. Look at the picture. What is the Amazon? Where is it?

2. Read about Elizabeth Grey's exciting and dangerous trip down the Amazon River.

3. 🔲 Listen to the rest of the interview and answer these questions.
a. How many people finished the trip?
b. Why didn't the others finish?
c. Was she afraid?
d. What did she get from this experience?

1 Words to Remember WF

1. Look for these words in the Wordfinder.

desert	hills	lake	mountains
rain forest	river	ocean	

2. Complete the names of the places. Do you know where they are?
a the Nile .....
b. the Andes .....
c. the Sahara .....
d. the Indian .....
e. ..... Titicaca

REPORTER: Why did you go on this expedition?

ELIZABETH: I was a secretary and I was bored with my job. Then I heard about a women's expedition on the Amazon, so I decided to leave my job and go.

REPORTER: When did the expedition begin?

ELIZABETH: It started in November, 1993.

REPORTER: Where did it start?

ELIZABETH: It started in the Andes Mountains in Peru.

REPORTER: When did the expedition finish?

ELIZABETH: It finished in April, 1994.

REPORTER: Where did it finish?

ELIZABETH: It finished in Belem, Brazil.

REPORTER: Who went with you?

ELIZABETH: Well, eight women started the expedition. There were three Americans; one was a doctor. There was also a woman from Japan, two from Canada, one from Mexico, and one from Venezuela. We had two women guides, a Colombian and a Brazilian.

2 Spotlight

1. Study the structures below.

Where When Why How	*did* you *go*?	To South America. Last year. Because I was bored. By plane.

Who	*went* with you?	My friends.

2. Compare the two kinds of questions. What is the subject in the first kind of question? What is the subject in the second kind of question? When is *did* not necessary?

3 Listening

Read the answers to the questions. Then listen to this interview with Will Larson, another adventurer, and write the questions.

a. ..... ? I went to Antarctica.
b. ..... ? We traveled across Antarctica by dogsled.
c. ..... ? There were six of us.
d. ..... ? No, I was the only American. The others were from China, France, Japan, Russia and England.
e. ...... ? We left on July 27, 1989.
f. ..... ? We traveled about 3,700 miles.
g. ..... ? It took seven months.
h. ..... ? Well, of course it was extremely cold. We also had to ski 20 miles a day.
i. ..... ? Yes, we all finished.

4 Practice

1. Imagine you have an interview with a famous explorer from the past. Write a past tense question for each answer.

a. ..... ?
My expedition sailed around the world.
b. ..... ?
The King of Spain gave me the money for the expedition.
c. ..... ?
We left in 1519.
d. ..... ?
I had five ships.
e. ..... ?
One ship returned to Spain.

2. What is the name of this famous explorer? See page 79 for the answer.

5 Talk in Pairs WF

Pretend that you went on an adventure. Decide where you went, when you went, what you did, and who went with you. Your partner will ask you questions. Then change roles.

6 Writing WF

Write your questions and your partner's answers from number 5.

a.

b.

c.

At the Start

1. Look at the pictures. Which person in each picture is giving advice?

2. Read the advice. What problem do you think each person has?
a. Maybe you should get a different job.
b. Maybe you should call the police.
c. You shouldn't stay out so late.

3. 🔲 Now listen to the conversations. Did you guess correctly?

1 Spotlight

1. Study the structures below.

I You He/She We They	*should* *shouldn't*	go.

2. Complete the sentences with *should* or *shouldn't*.
a. Students ..... study.
b. Young children ..... drink coffee.
c. Everyone ..... get some exercise.
d. You ..... tell other people's secrets.

2 Practice

Look at the picture below and give each person advice.

3 Talk in Pairs

Think of three problems. Tell your partner.
He/She will give you advice.

4 Reading

1. Read the article and choose the best title.
a. Friendship Around the World
b. How to be a Good Friend
c. Friendship and Health
d. Having Friends at Work

2. Answer *true* or *false*.
a. People with friends are always healthy.
b. Talking to someone can make you feel better.
c. Often adults think that friends aren't important.
d. You shouldn't talk to people that you don't know.

3. Match the words on the left with the meanings on the right.

1. elderly   a. good friend
2. extremely   b. become friends with someone
3. powerful   c. very
4. close friend   d. old
5. make friends   e. strong

5 Pronunciation

1. Read and listen to these words.
should   show   short   she   shout   shoot
shot   children   chance   chart   check
change   cheese   China

2. Listen to the words on the tape.
Do they begin with "sh" or "ch"?

3. Repeat these sentences.
a. Please show the charts to the children.
b. The man from China checked the cheese shop.
c. She was a short child.

"She's my best friend..." Children often say these words. Unfortunately, when we get older, work becomes more important and we often forget about friendship. Now, however, doctors say that friendship is **extremely** important for health. Studies show that people who have friends do not get sick as easily as people who do not have friends. In one study of 1,368 heart patients, people with friends lived longer than people without close friends or a husband or wife. One doctor said, "Having someone to talk to is very **powerful** medicine."

Another study of elderly people shows that the people with a husband or wife or **close** friends are healthier than people who are alone. Their bodies can fight disease better and they have lower levels of cholesterol. There are many other studies that show that people who are lonely get sick more often.

How can you make friends? Join groups or clubs. Look for people who seem lonely. Don't wait for people to come to you, take a chance and invite someone to have coffee or to study together. And remember, the best way to find friends is to be a friend. So **make friends** and stay healthy.

14

At the Start

1. Look at the pictures. Where do you think the diver found buried treasure?

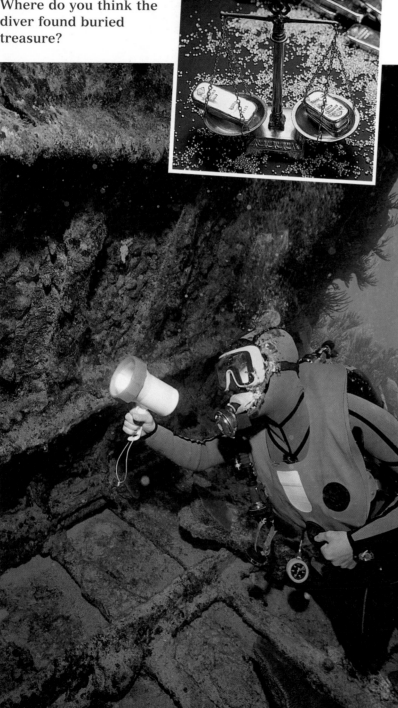

2. Read the article and answer the questions.

a. How many years ago did the SS *Central America* sink?

b. How many people died when the ship sank.

c. How much money did the three men spend to find the gold?

d. How much gold did they find?

GOLD!

For 131 years one of the world's richest treasures was lost on the bottom of the sea. It lay in the wreck of the 19th century ship, the SS *Central America*, which sank in a hurricane in September 1857. The treasure belonged to hundreds of California gold miners who died with their fortunes.

Until recently, the riches of the *Central America* were unreachable by man or machine, more than 2,500 meters below the surface of the ocean. Then, in 1985, three men – an engineer, a geologist and a journalist – began searching for the ship. Three years and $12,000,000 later, with the help of an undersea robot, the men found more than a billion dollars in gold.

1 Spotlight

1. Look at these phrases.

How much	milk? honey? homework?

How many	children? books? chairs?

2. Complete the sentences below with *countable* or *uncountable*.

a. *Milk, honey,* and *homework* are ..... nouns.

b. *Children, books,* and *chairs* are ..... nouns.

3. Complete this rule.

Use *how much* with ..... nouns.
Use *how many* with ..... nouns.

4. Use the rule to complete these questions.

a. ..... people live in your house?

b. ..... radios do you have in your house?

c. ..... stations do you listen to regularly?

d. ..... programs do you listen to?

e. ..... time do you spend listening to the radio?

2 Listening

Listen to this program on WXCB radio. Check your questions in *Spotlight*. Then listen again and write the five answers you hear.

3 Talk in Pairs WF

1. Complete the table to make up a story about a treasure that you found.

	Your story	Your partner's story
what/find		
where/find		
when/find		
how much/find		
how many years/search		
how much money/spend		

2. Ask your partner questions to complete the table for his/her story.

4 Writing

Write your story.

1. Talk to your classmates to find someone who:

a. went to a disco last weekend.

b. wrote a postcard yesterday.

c. often gets angry.

d. was at a supermarket yesterday.

e. took a bus to school today.

f. can help you with your homework.

2. Make questions to complete the following conversation.

RICKY: Nice to see you back at work, Jane. How was your vacation?

JANE: It was fantastic!

RICKY: [1] ..... ?

JANE: We went to some cabins up in the mountains near Lake Bonaventure.

RICKY: Oh yes. Someone told me about them [2] ..... ?

JANE: It takes about four hours. It's not too far.

RICKY: No, I guess not. [3] ..... ?

JANE: Oh we did just about everything. We swam, hiked, fished—I even went horse-back riding.

RICKY: [4] ..... ?

JANE: Believe it or not, I didn't fall off. I had a good horse. And guess what! We saw a huge bear!

RICKY: [5] ..... ?

JANE: Down by the river that goes into the lake.

RICKY: [6] ..... ?

JANE: Of course I was afraid.

RICKY: [7] ..... ?

JANE: What did we do? We didn't move an inch and after a few minutes he left.

RICKY: [8] ..... ?

JANE: We got home last night. That's why I'm so tired.

3. Unscramble the sentences and use capital letters where necessary.

a. shouldn't/money/your/spend/you/.

b. who/museum/went/you/to/the/with/?

c. your/come/friend/when/did/?

d. usually/bus/I/by/go/.

e. you/tomorrow/help/I'll/.

4. Substitute the correct pronoun for the underlined word or words.

a. Please tell <u>Mr. Burns</u> that I can't go to class today.

b. Our friends gave <u>Pete and me</u> a really nice party.

c. We didn't see <u>Jim and Betty</u> after class.

d. <u>John and I</u> didn't understand <u>the lesson</u>.

e. <u>Sally</u> gave <u>her mother</u> a sweater for her birthday.

5. **Find the errors in the sentences. Then correct them.**

a. Please ask she to call me.

b. Did you took out the garbage?

c. I'm sorry I forgot my homework. I bring it tomorrow.

d. We not went to the disco.

6. **Fill the blanks with the correct form of the verb.**

A: Hello, can I ¹ ..... to Gina please?
_{speak}

B: She ² ..... here right now. Who ³ ..... please?
_{be/not} _{call}

A: This is Lisa.

B: Oh hi Lisa. Gina ⁴ ..... around four o'clock.
_{leave}

A: Where ⁵ ..... she ....?
_{go}

B: I'm not sure but I think she ⁶ ..... to Connie's
_{go}

house. They ⁷ ..... study for a chemistry
_{have to}

exam.

A: What time ⁸ ..... she ..... back?
_{be}

B: She ⁹ ..... Lisa, but she ¹⁰ ..... get up early
_{not/say} _{have to}

tomorrow, so she shouldn't ¹¹ ..... home late.
_{get}

A: Well, thank you very much. I ¹² ..... back
_{call}

later then.

B: Okay Lisa, bye.

7. **Listen to the song and write in the missing words.**

❀❀❀ Today ❀❀❀

¹ ..... while ² ..... blossoms still cling ³ ..... the vine,

⁴ ..... taste your strawberries, I'll ⁵ ..... your sweet wine,

A ⁶ ..... tomorrows ⁷ ..... all pass away,

Before I ⁸ ..... , all the joy ⁹ ..... is mine–today.

¹⁰ ..... be a dandy ¹¹ ..... I'll ¹² ..... a rover,

¹³ ..... know who I ¹⁴ ..... by the song ¹⁵ ..... I sing,

I'll feast ¹⁶ ..... your table, ¹⁷ ..... sleep in your clover,

¹⁸ ..... cares what ¹⁹ ..... will bring.

Repeat Chorus

I ²⁰ ..... be contented with ²¹ ..... glory,

I can't ²² ..... on promises winter to ²³ ..... ,

²⁴ ..... is the moment and now is ²⁵ ..... story,

I'll ²⁶ ..... and I'll cry and I'll ²⁷ ..... .

15

At the Start

Match the pictures with the conversations.

a. "Oh no! I'm late! My bus comes at 6:57!"
   "Well hurry! Maybe you can catch it!"

b. "Oh no! Our ride isn't here!"
   "Let's call a taxi."

c. "Oh, the train is late again. Now I'll never get to work on time."
   "These trains always break down."

1 Words to Remember WF

Look at the forms of transportation in the Wordfinder. Then study the verbs below and make phrases like this:
miss the bus

miss   breakdown   take   catch   walk   drive
ride   go

> **!** We usually use *by* to talk about transportation.
> I go *by* car/bus.
> **The exception is:**
> I go *on foot.* I walk.

2 Listening

1. 🔲 Listen to the conversation. What forms of transportation did Mike try?

2. 🔲 Listen again. What was wrong with each form of transportation?

3 Talk in Pairs WF

Have conversations with your partner like this:
A: How do you get to *work*?
B: I usually *go by* car.
A: How long does it take?
B: It takes about *20 minutes.*
A: What time do you leave?
B: I leave about *8:30.*

4 Writing

Write about a bad experience with transportation similar to the conversation in *Listening*.

5 Reading

1. Quickly look at the article and find this information.

a. when Soichiro Honda began to make motorcycles

b. when he died

2. Look at the reading and put these events in order.

a. Honda started making motorcycles.

b. Soichiro Honda died.

c. Honda saw his first car.

d. Honda built the N360.

e. World War II ended.

f. He began to sell Hondas in the United States.

3. Look for these words in the reading. Then match them with their definitions.

1. passenger   a. motor
2. inspiration   b. any form of transportation
3. engine   c. more than
4. over   d. a person, not the driver, in a vehicle
5. vehicles   e. a good idea

Soichiro Honda

The Honda car was the **inspiration** of Soichiro Honda. Honda loved cars from the time he was six years old, when he saw a Ford Model T in the street of his town, near Hamamatsu, Japan. Before he was 18, he used an **engine** from an old American airplane and built his first car.

After World War II, Honda decided to make motorcycles. In 1948, he started his company in a small workshop in Tokyo. After his motorcycles became successful, Honda began to dream about making cars. His first **passenger** car was called the N360.

Eventually, Honda decided to try to sell cars in the United States. His cars soon became famous on the other side of the Pacific Ocean, too.

Soichiro Honda died in August 1991 but his company lives on. **Over** two million Honda cars, motorcycles and other **vehicles** are sold around the world every year.

16

At the Start

Match the traffic signs with their meanings.

one-way street   intersection   stop

1 Listening

1. Listen to the conversation. Find the answers to these questions.

a. Where does the woman want to go?

b. Can she walk to the post office?

2. Listen again and find these things on the map.

Clay Street   Preston Avenue   the Post Office
stop sign   traffic light

3. Listen again and mark the route that the man suggested.

2 Words to Remember

Label the diagrams with the words below.

north   south   east   west   left   right

no ..... turn   no ..... turn

3 Talk in Pairs

1. Look at the map. You are at the corner of State Street and Temple Street. Ask your partner how to get to two of these places by car:

Hansen Planetarium   the Public Library
Memorial Park   Webster Hotel

Example:

A: Excuse me. Could you tell me how to get to *Hansen Planetarium?*

B: Sure. *Go east two blocks on Temple Street. Turn right on Broad Street. Go south two blocks. Turn right on Adams. The planetarium is across from King's supermarket.*

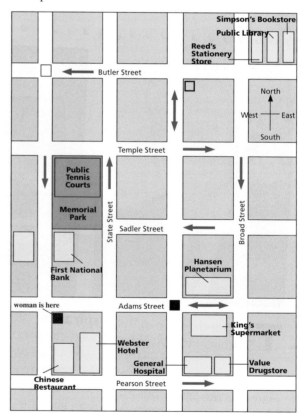

2. Write down the names of three places in your city. Ask your partner how to get there from your school.

4 Reading

1. Look at the diagram. Find the *dashboard, steering wheel, button, screen.*

2. Read the article. Answer true or false.
a. In a smart car you don't have to drive.
b. Smart cars save time.
c. In a smart car, the driver has to read the directions from a screen.
d. Smart cars are safer than normal cars.
e. Not many people are interested in making smart cars.

3. Look for the vocabulary words in the reading. Then match them with their definitions.
1. cure
2. get lost
3. destination
4. indicate
5. traffic
6. route

a. vehicles on the road
b. the way from one place to another
c. show
d. something that makes sick people healthy
e. the place where you are going
f. not able to find the way

Car Talk

I'm the kind of person that **gets lost** around the corner from my house. I thought that it was a sickness and there was no **cure**. But fortunately for me and other people like me, a cure is on the way – smart cars!

You can already get a smart car in some parts of the United States, Japan, Germany and the Netherlands. Each car has a touch screen computer on the dashboard. The driver enters his (or her) **destination** into the computer. And as soon as he starts off, he hears a friendly voice telling him, "Go west on Lakeview Drive. Turn right at the next intersection." A map appears on the screen. It shows the correct **route** in bright colors. The driver can also push a button on the steering wheel to ask for a traffic report. Then the screen will **indicate** areas of heavy **traffic**. It will suggest another route, if necessary. When the driver makes a wrong turn, the friendly voice of the computer doesn't get angry. It simply tells him another way to get to his destination.

A smart car is wonderful for people like me. However, it may also be great for people in general. It can help solve traffic problems and make the roads safer. This is why 18 carmakers and 124 research groups are working on ways to make smart cars available to more people.

Maybe soon, you and I will be able to drive to the supermarket without getting lost!

At the Start

🔊 Listen to this folk song on the tape.
Match the verses to the pictures.

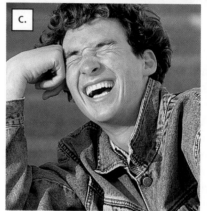

Kum-ba-ya

Verse 1
Someone's crying Lord*, Kum-ba-ya
Someone's crying Lord, Kum-ba-ya
Someone's crying Lord, Kum-ba-ya
Oh, Lord Kum-ba-ya

Verse 2
Someone's laughing Lord, Kum-ba-ya
(Repeat twice)
Oh, Lord Kum-ba-ya

Verse 3
Someone's singing Lord, Kum-ba-ya
(Repeat twice)
Oh, Lord Kum-ba-ya

Verse 4
Someone's working Lord, Kum-ba-ya
(Repeat twice)
Oh, Lord Kum-ba-ya

*Lord is another name for God.

1 Spotlight

1. Study the structures below.

I	*am*		*Am*	I		Yes, I am. / No, I'm not.
He She It	*is*	*(not) working.*	*Is*	he she it	*working?*	Yes, he is. / No, he isn't.
You We They	*are*		*Are*	you we they		Yes, we are. / No, we aren't.

2. Match the two columns.
1. She walks to the park.
2. She's walking to the park.
3. She walked to the park.

a. now
b. every day
c. yesterday

> ❗ You cannot contract
> positive short answers:
> *Yes, I am.* NOT *Yes, I'm.*

17

2 Practice

1. Look at the pictures. Say what the people are doing. Use these verbs:

help   play   feed   carry   talk

2. What do you think these people are doing right now? Write sentences about your father/your mother/your sister/your brother/your best friend.

3. Now tell your partner about them.

3 Listening

Listen to the conversation. Answer these questions.

a. Where does Martha have to go?
b. What is Help for Africa doing?
c. What does Bill say that he is doing?
d. What is he really doing?
e. What does he decide to do?

4 Talk in Pairs

Think of an occupation. Your partner will try to guess it.
Example:

A: What are you doing?

B: I'm writing. I'm giving someone a piece of paper.

A: Are you a teacher?

B: No. I'm standing in the street. I'm holding my hand up.

A: Are you a police officer?

B: Yes, I am.

5 Writing

You are on vacation. Write a postcard to a friend. Tell him or her what you are doing at the moment.
Example:

Dear Fred,

Well here I am in beautiful Hawaii. And what am I doing? I'm sitting in my hotel. Why? Because it's raining! I went to the beach yesterday morning and in the afternoon it started to rain. So I'm watching TV and writing postcards. And I'm thinking about all my friends back in sunny Chicago!

See you soon.

Chuck

18

At the Start

Look at the picture and try to answer these questions.

a. Which man was on the plane?
b. Do you think he had a good trip? Why or why not?

1 Listening

1. 📼 Listen and answer these questions.
a. Where is Dave?
b. Was there a movie on the plane?
c. Why didn't Dave eat on the plane?
d. What does Dave need?
e. Where does Dave have to go now?

2. 📼 Look at the adjectives in *Words to Remember*. Listen again and check the adjectives you hear.

2 Words to Remember   WF

1. Study these adjectives and verbs.

Adjectives		Verbs	
angry	frustrated	*be*	
bored	hungry	*get*	excited/dizzy
confused	thirsty	*feel*	
dizzy	worried		
excited	tired		
frightened			

2. Find an adjective to describe how you would feel in these situations.

a. You're learning to ice skate. This is your fifth lesson. You fall down every time you take two steps. *You feel ..... .*
b. A friend invited you to a lecture on nuclear physics. You don't know anything about nuclear physics. The lecture was three hours long. *You got very ..... .*
c. You're waiting for your daughter to come home. It's now 2 A.M. and she's three hours late. *You are ..... .*
d. You're about to leave for Europe. This is your first time outside your country and you saved for three years to take this trip. *You feel ..... .*

3 Talk in Pairs

Tell your partner about a time when you felt:

angry
bored
confused
excited
frightened
frustrated
worried

Example:
I felt bored in English class.
We had to ...

4 Reading

1. Look at the people in the pictures. Can you guess how they feel? Look at page 79 for the answers.

2. Match the words and the definitions.

1. gesture
2. kinesics
3. facial expression
4. hug
5. bow

a. to bend your body forward
b. a body movement that sends a message
c. to hold tightly in your arms
d. the study of non-verbal messages
e. the way your face looks

3. What do you think this person is saying with his body?

Body Language

We need words to tell people how we feel but we communicate our feelings in many other ways too; for example, with facial expressions. Do you know what the expressions below mean? Most cultures interpret these expressions in the same way.

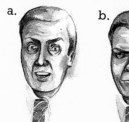

However, gestures often have different meanings in different cultures. Do you understand any of these gestures?

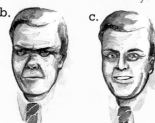

In many cultures, you have to make the right gestures before you can start the conversation. Sometimes you have to bow, hug, shake hands or kiss. Then and only then can a conversation begin..

Body position and the position of arms and legs communicate many things to a careful observer. What can you say about these people?

The study of body language is called kinesics. For example, scientists discovered that when a person sees something he likes, the pupil (the black part) of his eye gets bigger. Television advertising uses this idea. They study people's eyes while they are watching television. Then they can see which commercials they like best.

19

1.

At the Start

Look at the statements and pictures. Say which are true and which are false. Look at page 79 for the answers.

1. Dolphins are *faster* than sailfish.
2. Canada is *bigger* than China.
3. An elephant is *heavier* than a blue whale.
4. Diamonds are *more expensive* than gold.
5. The Mayan calendar system was *more complicated* than our calendar system.

1 Words to Remember

Look at the words in italics above. Find the opposites of the words below:

a. smaller
b. lighter
c. simpler
d. slower
e. cheaper

2.

Canada

4.

5.

3.

2 Spotlight

1. Study the forms below.

Group A	Group B	Group C
calm	intelligent	happy
calm**er**	*more* intelligent	happ**ier**

2. Look at the adjectives in *At the Start*. Divide the adjectives into three groups like the ones above.

3. Look at the groups and complete these rules about making comparatives.
a. For words of one syllable add ..... . (Sometimes you must also double the last letter).
b. For words of two or more syllables use .... .
c. For words that end in ..... , drop the ..... and add ..... .

> ! good—better
> ! bad—worse

3 Listening

1. 📼 Listen to two people talk about cars and motorcyles. What are the six comparative adjectives that you hear?

2. Now use the adjectives to make sentences comparing cars and motorcyles.
Example:
A car is bigger than a motorcycle.

4 Pronunciation

📼 Listen and repeat these sentences. Notice the pronunciation of the word *than*.
a. She's more intelligent than Carla.
b. Your car is bigger than his car.
c. Sometimes children are smarter than their parents.
d. Los Angeles is nearer than San Francisco.
e. We're more careful than they are.

5 Practice

1. Write the comparative form of these adjectives.

a. cheap	e. easy	i. intelligent
b. friendly	f. delicious	j. interesting
c. pretty	g. slow	k. small
d. weak	h. hot	l. uncomfortable

2. Use the adjectives above to compare these things.
a. an elephant/a turtle
b. children/adults
c. a bicycle/a car
d. spaghetti/a hamburger
e. cats/dogs
f. country life/city life
g. black/yellow
h. your language/ English
i. summer/winter
j. math/geography

6 Talk in Groups

Think of something that you like. Then think of something in the same category that you don't like. Talk to your classmates like this:
A: I like English but I don't like French.
B: Why?
A: Because English is easier.

7 Writing

Write your opinions and the opinions of your classmates from *Talk in Groups*.

20

At the Start

Look at the picture. Describe the clerk. Describe the customer.

2 Words to Remember WF

1. Look at the Wordfinder and label the clothes below.

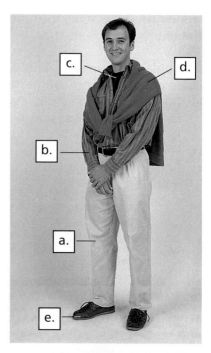

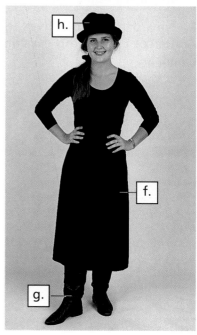

1 Listening

1. 📼 Look at the photos. Listen to the conversation between the clerk and the customer. What does the woman want?

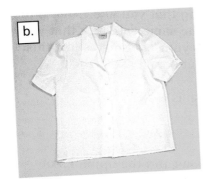

2. Answer the questions.
a. What color does she want?
b. What size does she want?
c. Why is the clerk surprised?

2. Look at the expressions below and complete the conversation.

Clerk   Customer

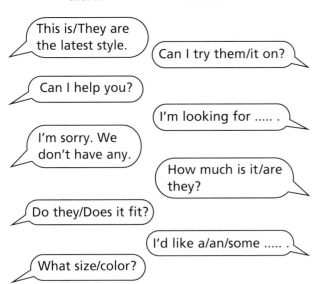

This is/They are the latest style.

Can I try them/it on?

Can I help you?

I'm looking for ..... .

I'm sorry. We don't have any.

How much is it/are they?

Do they/Does it fit?

I'd like a/an/some ..... .

What size/color?

! Some clothes, like *pants* or *shorts* are always plural. Others, like *shoes* or *gloves* are usually plural. For all these, use *some* or *a pair of*.

A: Good morning. ¹..... ?
B: Yes, ²..... some white pants.
A: Of course. ³..... ?
B: Thirty-four, I think.
A: These are very nice. And they're ⁴..... .
B: ⁵..... ?
A: Sure, the dressing room is right over there.
    (*5 minutes later*)
A: ⁶..... ?
B: They fit fine. ⁷..... ?
A: $200.
B: $200! I don't think I like them that much.

3 Role Play

Student A: You are a salesclerk.
Student B: You are a customer.
Have a conversation like the one above.

4 Reading

1. Look at the picture. Why do the jeans have holes in them?

Dressed to Kill

Many people watch fashion shows and look through magazines to get ideas of how to dress. But Patty Ludwin started a new fashion in a different way.

The idea for Patty Ludwin's creation came from a friend. The friend, Natalie, got very angry with **her** boyfriend. **She** was so angry that she wanted to shoot him. Instead of shooting **him**, she took his jeans and shot holes in them. The boyfriend didn't get angry when he saw his jeans. On the contrary, he loved them!

Patty now takes jeans and shoots **them** with 150 bullets. Each pair of jeans then has 300 holes. Are jeans more expensive with or without holes? With holes, of course!

Patty also makes jewelry, necklaces, earrings and bracelets out of bullets. She "signs" her creations with a picture of a bull's-eye and a bullet. Right now she only sells by mail but she hopes that soon she will be able to sell her jeans and jewelry in stores. **You** can order a catalog by writing to:

Calamity Jeans and Jewels
301 Cricketwood Court
Canonsburg, PA   15317

2. Answer true or false.
a. Patty Ludwin was angry at her boyfriend.
b. Patty's friend shot her boyfriend.
c. Patty sells jeans with or without bullet holes.
d. Patty makes jeans and jewelry.

3. What do these words refer to?
a. her   **b.** she   **c.** him   **d.** them   **e.** you

At the Start

Read the statements. Match them with the pictures.

The biggest, the longest, the tallest ...

1. Ice hockey is *the fastest* sport. The puck often travels at more than 160 km per hour.

2. Many people think that the VW bug is *the most dependable* car in the world. Perhaps that is why it was also *the most popular* car ever built. Despite its dependability and popularity, it is also one of *the cheapest* cars ever built.

3. *The largest* soccer stadium in the world is in Mexico City. It holds 100,000 people.

4. Frank Lloyd Wright was one of America's *best* and *most imaginative* architects. He designed the Guggenheim Museum in New York.

5. Dogs are probably *the most loyal* animals in the world. There are many stories of dogs saving their master's lives.

6. The Atacama Desert in Chile is *the driest* place on Earth. In 1971 it rained for the first time in 400 years.

1 Words to Remember

1. Look in the statements and find the words to complete the table.

Adjectives	Nouns	Verbs
	imagination	imagine
	loyalty	xxxxxxxxx
		depend on
popular		xxxxxxxxx

2. Complete these sentences with the correct word from the table in number 1.
a. Many people believe that you can ..... a VW bug.
b. Can you ..... how the world will change in 100 years?
c. Hamburgers are very ..... around the world.
d. Don't ask Harry to do anything. He's not ..... at all.
e. She's a very ..... friend.

21

2 Spotlight

1. Study the superlative adjectives below.

Group A	Group B	Group C
Hockey is *the fastest* game.	It is *the most popular* car.	It was *the prettiest* dress.

> **!** *good/better/best*
> *bad/worse/worst*

2. Look for the superlative adjectives in *At the Start*. Divide them into three groups like the ones above.

3. Look at your lists and complete these rules about making superlatives.
a. For words of one syllable add [1]..... .
b. For words of two syllables use [2]..... .
c. For words that end in [3] ..... , drop the [4] ..... and add [5] ..... .

3 Listening

1. Listen to a boss deciding which employee to fire. Use these words to describe Bob, Ted, Carol and Alice.
dependable imaginative loyal old new

2. Now decide who you think the boss will fire. Give reasons for your answer.

4 Practice

Complete the sentences with superlative adjectives to make true sentences. Use each word in the box once.

> long   high   small   near   large
> famous   difficult   tall   fast

a. The CN Tower in Toronto is the ..... building in the world.
b. Mt. Everest is the ..... mountain in the world.
c. The sun is not the ..... star in the universe but it is the ..... to Earth.
d. John F. Kennedy was one of the ..... presidents in the U.S.
e. The Vatican is the ..... country in the world.
f. The cheetah is the ..... animal on land.
g. The ..... bridge in the world is the Ponchartrain Causeway in Louisiana. It is more than 38 km long.
h. Many people think that chess is the ..... game to play.

5 Talk in Pairs

Look at these pictures with your partner. Which is the best, most interesting, etc.?

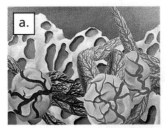

6 Writing

Write about the pictures in 5. Explain which one you like best and why.
I like picture B the best because....

At the Start

1. Look at the cards in this picture. Do people play cards with them? Who uses them?

2. Read this conversation between a fortune teller and her client.

M.ZARA: This first card is called the lovers. This card means that you are going to make a decision and perhaps it's going to be a difficult decision.

LEO: Am I going to leave my job?

M.ZARA: I'm not sure. I only know it's not going to be an easy decision. Hmm. The second card is the five of cups.

LEO: What does that mean?

M.ZARA: It means that you're going to feel bad about your decision.

LEO: Feel bad?

M.ZARA: Yes, but don't worry, because the third card, temperance, shows that in the end, you are going to accept your decision and you are going to be OK.

LEO: Well, that's a relief.

3. Look at the fortune teller's predictions. Which ones are good?

1 Spotlight

1. Study the stuctures below.

I He/She You We They	am is are	going to take a trip.

2. Look at the box and complete the sentences.

a. I am ..... to leave tomorrow.
b. She ..... going to take an exam.
c. We are going ..... have lunch at 12.
d. It is ..... to rain today.

3. Now look at the sentences in 2 and make them negative. Use contractions.

Example: *You aren't going to work tomorrow.*
You're not going to work tomorrow.

2 Listening

1. 📼 Look at the list of predictions below. Then listen to a fortune teller reading Carol's palm. Which positive or negative predictions does she make?

a. have a visitor
b. make a lot of money
c. lose your job
d. have four children
e. find a new boyfriend
f. get married
g. move to another city
h. make a lot of new friends
i. be sick
j. find a new career

2. Make sentences using the information above.

Carol is/isn't going to ..... .

Carol and Brad are/aren't going to ..... .

3 Practice

Look at the pictures and use the words in the box to say what is going to happen.

> ! *going to* is usually pronounced "gonna"

take a trip	go swimming	not play tennis
have an exam	break	rain

1.
2.
3.
4.
5.
6.

4 Talk in Pairs

Ask your partner about his/her plans:

when this course is over
next weekend
on his/her next vacation
after class today

Example:
A: What are you going to do *when this class is over?*
B: I'm going to *register for the next class.*

5 Writing

Write about your future plans:

when this class is over
on your next vacation
next weekend
after class today

Review 3: Units 15–22

1. Write questions for the answers.

a. ..... ?

She's washing her hair.

b. ..... ?

Yes, I think he's going to buy it.

c. ..... ?

I really feel angry.

d. ..... ?

Turn right at the next corner and go down three blocks.

e. ..... ?

Pete Mitchell is the best.

2. Fill in the blanks with the correct form of the verb.

A: Hey Ted, what ¹ ..... you ² ..... ?
_{do}

B: Something's wrong with my brother's bike and I ³ ..... it.
_{fix}

A: Looks pretty good to me, Ted. I ⁴ ..... to ask
_{come}
you something.

⁵ ..... you ⁶ ..... to go to a baseball game?
_{want}

B: When?

A: This afternoon. Mike's team ⁷ ..... on that
_{play}
new baseball diamond at the Civic Center.

B: I don't know. How many of the guys ⁸ ..... ?
_{go}

A: Joe, Sam, Tim almost everybody. You

should ⁹ ..... .
_{go}

B: But I really ¹⁰ ..... a lot of work to do.
_{have}

A: C'mon Ted. You can ¹¹ ..... your work
_{do}
tomorrow.

B: Okay, I ¹² ..... you there.
_{see}

3. 1. 🔲 Look at the map, listen to the conversation and trace the route the man suggested.

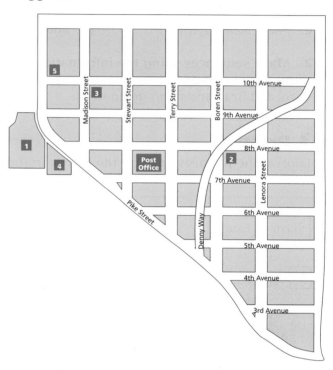

2. Find these places on the map.

a. the woman's position

b. Shoreline Community College

c. Highland Park

d. the Westin Hotel

e. City Hall

3. Answer these questions.

a. How is the woman going to go to the hotel?

b. How can she go to City Hall?

4. Write directions to tell the woman how to get to the post office from the hotel.

4. Find the errors and correct them.

a. They are watch TV.

b. This book was interestinger than the last one.

c. She is the most fast runner in the school.

d. The bank is in the left side of the street.

e. What are they going buy at the supermarket?

5. Unscramble the words to make sentences or questions.

a. it/long/take/how/does/?

b. get/plane/the/I/dizzy/always/on/.

c. more/is/English/I/think/than/French/ difficult/.

d. like/please/size/I'd/fourteen/.

e. usually/bus/I/by/go/.

f. the/expensive/this/store/watch/the/most/ in/is/.

6. Mr. and Mrs. Clark want to buy a dog for their daughter. This is the information they have from the store about the different kinds of dogs.

	St. Bernard	German shepherd	Chihuahua
full weight	75-82kg	27-39kg	3-5kg
cost	$500	$250	$325
present age	2 months	5 months	7 months
Qualities noisy obedient	✱ ✱ ✱	✱ ✱ ✱ ✱ ✱	✱ ✱ ✱ ✱

✱ a little   ✱✱ very   ✱✱✱ very very

Chihuahua

Saint (St.) Bernard

German Shepherd

Complete the sentences with the correct comparative or superlative.

a. The St. Bernard is ..... than the German _{heavy} Shepherd. And the Chihuahua is the ..... of _{light} the three.

b. The St. Bernard is the ..... and the ..... of the _{expensive} _{young} three.

c. The Chihuahua is ..... than the German _{small} Shepherd but it is ..... . _{expensive}

d. The ..... of the three is the German _{obedient} Shepherd, but the St. Bernard is ..... than _{obedient} the Chihuahua.

e. The German Shepherd is ..... than the St. _{noisy} Bernard, but of course, the Chihuahua is the ..... of the three. _{noisy}

Optional Exercises and Activities

Unit 1

1. Look at the chart and make sentences about what these people do.

	Craig	Michelle
do homework	*****	*
go to class on time	—	**
pay attention in class	**	***
speak English in class	****	*
get good grades	****	—

Scale: (never) — → ***** (always)

2. Work in pairs.
Student A: Use the words below to make questions to ask Student B. Answer Student B's questions with *always, usually, often, sometimes, rarely, never.*

does   do   you   your mother   our teacher
watch   work   get up early   clean
read the newspaper   English   cook
television   in the morning   breakfast
every day

Student B: Use the words below to make questions to ask Student A. Answer Student A's questions with *always, usually, often, sometimes, rarely, never.*

does   do   you   your father   our teacher
study   go   to class   exercise   dancing
early   in the afternoon   late   eat meat
every day   to the movies

3.  Listen to these yes/no questions. Does the voice go up or down at the end? Then listen again and repeat.

a. Do you like school?

b. Is that Greg?

c. Are you a healthy person?

d. Does Barry study French?

Unit 2

1. Complete the sentences with *a/an, some* or *any.*

A: Excuse me sir. I need [1] ..... gas. Do you have [2] ..... ?

B: I'm sorry. I don't have [3] ..... extra gas but I can take you to a gas station.

A: Oh, I can't leave my car. I have [4] ..... expensive things inside and the doors don't have [5] ..... locks.

B: Well, do you have [6] ..... gas can? I can bring you [7] ..... gas.

A: Yes, I do. Here it is. Do you have [8] ..... change? I only have [9] ..... $100 bill.

B: I have [10] ..... money, but I don't have enough money to buy gas, so I certainly don't have change for $100!

A: Well, I don't know you. How can I give you $100?

B: I have [11] ..... idea. You take my car. Go buy the gas and I can wait here with your car.

A: Thanks a lot!

POLICEMAN: Tell me that story again! You gave your car to [12] ..... complete stranger!

2. Draw a picture with many different animals. Your partner will try to guess what animals are in the picture.

Example:

A: *Are there any cats in your picture?*

B: *Yes, there are some cats.*

3. Find the errors and correct them. Some sentences have no errors.

a. They don't have some ice cream.

b. We don't need any money.

c. Do you have any books?

d. There aren't some students in the classroom.

e. Is there some dangerous animals in the zoo?

f. He would like some tea?

g. There are some talking cockatoos.

Unit 3

1. Look at the pictures. Tell your partner about the people. Talk about:

facts	guesses
hair color	age
body type (tall/short fat/thin etc.)	occupation
	nationality
clothes	personality

a.   b.   c.   d.

2. Find the errors and correct them.

a. Marta has blond hair short.   *Marta has short blond hair*

b. Bill is fat, tall.   *tall and fat*

c. Christine has hair long, curly and black.   *long curly ~~and~~ black hair*

d. My brother has short, straight, brown hair.   *has*

e. Pat ~~is~~ short ~~and~~ curly.   *hair*

f. My father's ~~hair~~ is bald.

g. Samantha has eyes blue and curly hair.   *blue eyes and curly hair*

h. Cindy has ~~tall~~ black hair.   *long*

i. Bruce is with brown eyes and short blonde hair.   *Bruce ~~is~~ has brown eyes and short blonde hair.*

j. Caroline is black hair and straight.   *has straight, black hair*

Unit 4

1. Fill in the blanks with *has to, have to, doesn't have to, don't have to, can* or *can't*.

a. You ..... walk to school today. The weather is terrible.

b. She ..... work from two to eleven and she gets very tired.

c. Bill ..... work today. It's a holiday.

d. I ..... go to the movies tonight. I'm very busy.

e. It's four o'clock. Time to go home. We ..... do this tomorrow.

f. I ..... do some research so I ..... do my homework in the library. I ..... work at home. We don't have the books I need.

g. You ..... write a complete sentence. A short answer is fine.

h. We ..... have lunch at Gorky's. It's not expensive.

happy, sad interesting

2. Student A: You are not a very nice boss. Have a conversation with your employee, Student B, using *have to, can't* and *can* with these expressions.

have to can't can	work more hours go home later train the new employees have a coffee break have only half an hour for lunch— not an hour use the office telephone take a salary cut

Student B: You are Student A's employee. Have a conversation with your boss using *can, can't, don't* and *have to* with these expressions.

can can't have to	stay later than 6 P.M. go home for lunch stay home when your child is sick have a raise call your house to check on your son/daughter

Unit 5

1. With your partner, put the following conversation in order.

MR. MURPHY: Good afternoon doctor.

DOCTOR: Well now, do you have a headache too?

DOCTOR: And your throat?

DOCTOR: Hello Mr. Murphy. How are you today?

DOCTOR: Well, I think I have just the medicine for you.

MR. MURPHY: Yes, that's right doctor.

MR. MURPHY: Yes I do.

MR. MURPHY: Not too good, I'm afraid. I have a fever.

MR. MURPHY: It's very sore.

DOCTOR: Sore throat, headache and fever. Is that right?

Now make up a similar conversation with your partner.

2. Fill in the blanks with the correct word.

a. Do you have an aspirin? I have a ..... .

b. Jim has a bad ..... . I think he needs a hard bed.

c. A: Aaah-choo!
   B: Goodness! You have a terrible ..... .

d. Little Billy is very hot. I think he has a ..... .

e. I can't talk very well. I have a ..... .

3. Read the doctor's advice and correct it.

a. DOCTOR: What's the matter, Mr. Lopez?
   MR. LOPEZ: I have a headache and a fever.
   DOCTOR: You should drink honey, lemon juice and sleep on a hard bed.

b. DOCTOR: What's the problem, Ms. Tan?
   MS. TAN: I have a terrible sore throat.
   DOCTOR: Well. Drink only tea and toast for the next 24 hours.

c. DOCTOR: You look sick, Barbara.
   BARBARA: I feel sick. I have a very bad cold.
   DOCTOR: Take aspirin and do a lot of exercise.

d. DOCTOR: What's the matter, Martin?
   MARTIN: I have a backache.
   DOCTOR: Take vitamin C and eat only hot foods.

Unit 6

1. Play grammar tic-tac-toe with a partner. One person is X, the other is O. Choose a word. Make a sentence. If the sentence is correct put an X or an O in the box. If you think your partner is wrong, ask your teacher. The first person to get three X's or O's in a line wins.

were	we	who
is	your	was
at home	she	last week

I	yesterday	they
was	were	my
are	when	you

2. With a partner, look at the two pictures. Find the difference between where the things were yesterday and where they are today.

3. 📼 Listen to the four sentences. Do you hear *where* or *were*? Then listen again and repeat.

Unit 7

1. Read the paragraph below.

Every morning I get up at 7:00. I go down to the kitchen and I make some coffee. I drink my coffee, eat some toast and then I get dressed. At 8:00 I walk to the drugstore and I buy a newspaper. I wait at the bus stop in front of the drugstore and I catch the 8:15 bus. I get to the office at 8:30.

Now rewrite it in the past tense. Begin with *Yesterday I ..... .*

2. Work with a partner. Use your imagination to put the pictures in order and make up a story in the past.

3. Now draw your own pictures. Exchange with your partner. Write a story for his/her pictures.

4. Look at the timeline. Write sentences about the life of Malcolm X in the past tense.

1925	1946	1952	1964	1965
is born	goes to prison	leaves prison and became a Black Muslim Minister	goes to Mecca	dies

Unit 8

1. These are two mixed-up telephone conversations. Find the conversations and put them in the correct order.

a. Hello, is Mr. Brandon there please?

b. Just ask her to call Mike.

c. This is Peter Williams at Industrial Electronics.

d. Hello, can I speak to Jenny?

e. No. It's 555-1234.

f. Of course. I'll tell him when he comes back.

g. Can I leave a message?

h. Yes. Would you ask him to call me?

i. Okay Mike, I'll have her call you when she gets in.

j. Thank you. Goodbye.

k. Sure.

l. No, I'm sorry he isn't. Who's calling please?

m. Sorry. She's not in.

n. Does she have your phone number, Mike?

o. Would you like to leave a message, Mr. Williams?

2. Choose the correct pronouns.

a. We/Us saw they/them last night.

b. I/Me gave the new books to he/him.

c. Does she/her visit she/her every week?

d. Can they/them go with we/us?

e. He/Him doesn't have they/them.

3. Answer the question. Use the correct object pronoun in your answer.

a. Do you have my pen?
No , ...

b. Did Carol write the thank-you letters?
Yes, ...

c. Can I have that piece of cake?
Sure, ...

d. Did you see your mother this morning?
Yes ..... .

e. Does your brother always drive you and your sister to school?
Yes ..... .

f. Did Mrs. Philips teach Rodney in first grade?
No, ...

g. Can I help you with this problem?
Yes, ...

h. Do you call Betty every day?
No ..... .

Unit 9

1. Find the mistakes in the questions and answers below. Then correct them.

a. Did she worked with you?   Yes, she did.

b. Did he went?   No, he didn't.

c. Did they watched the television?   Yes, they did.

d. Did you want the money?   Yes, I wanted.

e. Does we told them?   Yes, we did.

2. Use the verbs below to make past tense questions. You may have to change the verb to the base form.

began	lived	studies	taught	got
work	eats	made	sweep	cut

3. Work in pairs.
Student B: Look at page 69.
Student A: Look at the information in the Information Box and answer Student B's questions about Carol.

Information Box

a. Carol lived in New York City in 1992.

b. She was a waitress.

c. She had a boyfriend named Mark.

d. Mark and Carol often went to the beach.

e. Carol was an excellent swimmer.

f. She saved a young boy's life.

Now ask Student B if these statements about Dave are true.

Example:
Was Dave a student in 1990?

g. Dave was a student in 1990.

h. He studied accounting at the University of Chicago.

i. He was an excellent student.

j. He graduated in 1993.

k. He got a great job.

l. He got married last year.

Unit 10

1. Work with a partner to complete the conversation. Compare your conversations with your classmates.

A: Oh dear. I dropped your [1] ..... .
B: Did it [2] ..... ?
A: Yes, it [3] ..... .
B: Oh no! My mother is going to kill me. That [4] ..... was [5] ..... .
A: Uh-oh. Well, I'll [6] ..... .
B: But you can't. It's [7] ..... .
A: Well, I'll [8] ..... .
B: I don't think you can. It was very [9] ..... .

2. Think of a problem that your partner can help you with. Then your partner will tell you what he/she will do to help you.

Example:
A: *I don't understand my English homework.*
B: *I'll explain it to you.*
or
A: *I forgot my lunch.*
B: *I'll give you part of my lunch.*

3. Have conversations about these situations.

Situation 1: Student A borrowed Student B's favorite tape and lost it!
Situation 2: Student B just spilled a cup of coffee on Student A's new shirt/dress.

4. 📟 Listen and choose the sentence you hear. Then listen again and repeat.

a. I'll leave at three.
I leave at three.

b. I'll live with Sue.
I live with Sue.

c. They'll let me go.
They let me go.

d. They'll laugh at us.
They laugh at us.

e. You'll like them
You like them.

Unit 11

1. Look at the statements. All of them are false. Say what's wrong and correct them.

Example:
Galileo didn't discover gravity. Newton discovered gravity.

a. Galileo discovered gravity.

b. Men went to the moon in 1989.

c. Columbus discovered Australia.

d. ET came from the moon.

e. Sylvester Stallone starred in the Terminator movies.

f. The 1994 World Cup was in Brazil.

g. Marco Polo travelled to Africa.

h. Einstein lived in the 16th century.

2. With your partner make up a story about a day when everything went wrong. Write as many sentences with *didn't* as you can. Begin like this:

Yesterday was a terrible day. First Margaret didn't get up on time. Then...

Now share the story with your class.

Unit 12

1. Look at the answers and write logical questions.

a. A: ..... ?   B: I ate a lot of pizzas.

b. A: ..... ?   B: I ate 55 large pizzas.

c. A: ..... ?   B: Because I wanted to be a record-holder.

d. A: ..... ?   B: It took about eight hours.

e. A: ..... ?   B: Last month.

f. A: ..... ?   B: My friends watched me.

g. A: ..... ?   B: I felt pretty sick.

2. Complete this paragraph about yourself.

Last year I ..... on vacation. It was ..... . I ..... . I ..... every day. I never ..... . I was ..... . This year I hope I ..... .

Now ask your partner questions about a place that they visited last year. Use *where, when, who, how,* etc. Then write another paragraph about your partner's vacation.

3. Think of five different roles you have in your life (sister, student, brother, babysitter, driver). Write a question for each role. Give your roles and your questions to your partner. Let him/her ask you the questions. You tell him/her the answers.

Example:

A: Who do you babysit for?

B: I babysit for dogs. I'm a dog sitter!

Unit 13

1. Complete the sentences with *should, shouldn't, will, can, can't.*

a. Children ..... play in the street. It's dangerous.

b. I practice every day but I still ..... speak Spanish well.

c. A: ..... I watch television?
   B: Of course you ..... .

d. You ..... smoke. It's bad for your health.

e. A: ..... I go to the doctor?
   B: I think it's a good idea.

f. I ..... study but I want to go to the movies.

g. You ..... leave when you want to.

h. Babies ..... talk very well.

i. I ..... fix your bicycle this afternoon, I promise.

2. Some people have bad habits. What advice can you give people who:

a. bite their nails

b. always lose their keys

c. are never on time

d. tap their fingers while they are talking

e. play loud music while people are sleeping

3. Fill in the blanks with appropriate advice.

a. Rob feels sick. He should ..... .

b. The students have a test tomorrow. They should ..... .

c. It's very late. We should ..... .

d. It's raining. You shouldn't ..... .

e. I'm too fat. I shouldn't ..... .

Unit 14

1. Write questions for these answers. Use *how much* or *how many.*

a. 65 kilos

b. two brothers and five sisters

c. About $50.

d. About two months.

e. Three: a Ford, a Mercedes and a Toyota.

f. All of it.

g. About 100 and they were all my friends.

h. Ten dogs, five cats, three birds and a crocodile.

2. Ask your partner questions to complete the questionnaire.

a. ..... hours a day do you study?

b. ..... classes do you have?

c. ..... free time do you have each day?

d. ..... homework do you get each day?

e. ..... hours do you work?

3. Look for the past tense of these verbs in the irregular verbs list on page 80.

present	past
see	_____
spend	_____
find	_____
sink	_____
send	_____

4. Complete the sentences with the past tense of the verbs above.

a. The ship ..... during a storm.

b. Sorry I can't go on vacation with you. I ..... all my money on a new stereo.

c. It's my lucky day! I just ..... $5!

d. I ..... a letter to Howard.

Unit 15

1. Think of as many kinds of transportation as you can. Put them into as many of these categories as you can.

land transportation
sea transportation
air transportation
two-wheeled transportation
four-wheeled transportation
public transportation
private transportation

2. Find the word that doesn't belong.

a.	talk	walk	drive	ride
b.	car	truck	table	bike
c.	arm	leg	hand	person
d.	wash	need	cook	clean
e.	her	him	we	them
f.	want	ate	taught	went
g.	tall	short	fat	intelligent

3. Ask a classmate questions to complete this chart. Use *how, how much, how far, how long*. Then tell your class the answers.

School Transportation Survey
kind of transportation
cost
distance
gas
time

Unit 16

1. Read the conversation. Then complete it.

A: Can you tell me how to get to the railway station?
B: [1] ..... .
A: Did you say turn left or right?
B: [2] ..... .
A: What do I do then?
B: [3] ..... .
A: Is it a one-way street?
B: [4] ..... .
A: What do I do then?
B: [5] ..... .
A: Thanks a lot.

2. Work in pairs. Student B: Look at page 69. Student A: Look at this map of New York City. You are at the corner of Fifth Avenue and 48th Street. Ask Student B how to get to:

a. Grand Central Station
b. the Museum of Modern Art
c. St. Patrick's Cathedral

3. Now choose two destinations from the map you used in exercise 2 and write the directions from 44th St. and Avenue of the Americas.

Unit 17

1. Complete the sentences with the present simple or present continuous form of the verb.

a. Mary usually ¹ ..... dinner but today ² ..... her birthday, so her
_{cook} _{be}
husband Mike ³ ..... dinner. He always ⁴ ..... dinner on her
_{cook} _{make}
birthday. Today he ⁵ ..... lasagna. It ⁶ ..... Mary's favorite
_{make} _{be}
dish.

b. Betty and Susan always ¹ ..... television between six and
_{watch}
seven. They ² ..... to watch the news. But today they ³ .....
_{like} _{not watch}
television. The television ⁴ ..... broken and they ⁵..... to fix it.
_{be} _{try}
Betty ⁶ ..... the antenna and Susan ⁷..... the controls.
_{move} _{turn}

2. Look at this picture with your partner. Find ten things that people are doing. Compare your answers with the class.

3. Play grammar tic-tac-toe. See optional exercise 1 in Unit 6 if you need help.

writing	drive	does
Tom	am	reading
book	is	I

Jane	working	are
now	laughing	they
teaching	here	is

Unit 18

1. How many words do you know to describe how you feel? Put them in as many of these categories as you can.

physical   pleasant   unpleasant

2. Match these columns.

1. confused.   **a.** You find a black widow spider in your bed.

2. dizzy   **b.** You can't do your math homework.

3. frustrated   **c.** Someone hits your new car.

4. frightened   **d.** You are trying to understand someone who doesn't speak your language.

5. angry   **e.** You are watching something go round and round.

3. Complete the following statements. Compare your answers with your partner.

a. I always feel frustrated when ..... .

b. I get angry when ..... .

c. I feel frightened when ..... .

d. I get really bored when ..... .

e. I often get confused when ..... .

Unit 19

1. Find the mistakes in these sentences and correct them.

a. Her house is big than my house.

b. Trains are more fast than cars.

c. Elephants are stronger then horses.

d. She's older than am I.

e. You're prettyer than she is.

2. With your partner compare the items below. Draw lines to show which items you compared. Make as many comparisons as you can.

Example:
A truck is heavier than a car.

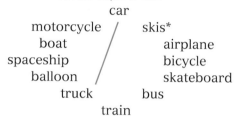

```
                        car
        motorcycle   /   skis*
           boat     /      airplane
        spaceship  /        bicycle
           balloon /        skateboard
                truck     bus
                   train
```

* Be careful —skis are plural!

3. Look at the survey of movie theaters in *Moviegoers Magazine*. Write four sentences comparing the Odeon and Tivoli Movie Theaters.

	Odeon Movie Theater	Tivoli Movie Theater
age	1935	1960
ticket price	$5.00	$8.50
comfort	✱✱	✱✱✱✱
size	500 seats	250 seats

Unit 20

1. Unscramble the conversations.

Conversation 1

Student A

A: Can I help you?

A: Here's one.

A: We have some very nice sweaters.

A: It's $75.

A: What size?

A: What would he like?

Student B

B: Yes, they are.

B: That's a bit expensive, I'm afraid.

B: He's about a 42, I think.

B: Can I see some?

B: I'm not sure. He needs a new sweater.

B: Yes, I need a birthday present for my father.

B: That's nice. How much is it?

Conversation 2

Student A

A: What size do you wear?

A: They're $250.

A: Can I help you?

A: These black ones are quite nice.

A: What kind of shoes?

Student B

B: Dressy shoes, to wear to a party.

B: Six and a half.

B: I'm looking for a pair of shoes.

B: I'm sorry. They're much too expensive.

B: Oh, they're lovely. How much are they?

2. Look at the pictures of these clothes. Tell your partner what you like and what you don't like about them.

3. Have a race with your partner to unscramble the words below. Find one piece of clothing that you can't wear with the others.

men's clothes	women's clothes
nteisn hesso	lusobe
htrsi-t	sesrd
eit	tksri
awestre	hesos
njase	aktecj
kssoc	

Unit 21

1. Use the ideas in parentheses to make a sentence about the item that is *the most* ....

Example:
(small) elephant, insect, bird

An insect is the smallest of the three.

a. (intelligent) chimpanzee, cow, mouse

b. (nice place for a vacation) mountains, beach, forest

c. (good place to live) city, small town, farm

d. (easy to take care of) babies, three-year-old children, eight-year-old children

e. (interesting) science fiction movies, mystery movies, romantic movies

f. (delicious) Chinese food, Italian food, French food

g. (big) New York City, Tokyo, Mexico City

2. With your partner, rate these things on a scale of one (the most) to six (the least). Then compare your answers with other members of your class.

	dangerous	expensive	boring	fast	easy	enjoyable
basketball						
soccer						
golf						
bowling						
tennis						
skiing						

3. Ask your partner questions about things that he/she has. Use these adjectives and follow the example.

A: What is the *nicest* thing you have?
B: I'm not sure. Probably *a ring that my father gave me.*

nice   important   expensive   big   small

Unit 22

1. Unscramble these sentences.

a. bookstore/go/going/she/to/tomorrow/the/is/to/.

b. your/going/aren't/you/pass/exam/math/to/.

c. is/to/who/Paris/going/you/go/to/with/?

d. he/live/going/where/to/is/?

e. today/not/are/going/come/they/to/.

2. Play grammar tic-tac-toe with a partner. See number 14 if you need help.

is	we	study
go	going	are
friend	buy	disco

I	children	they
is	need	help
New York	mother	you

3. 🖾 Listen and repeat these sentences.

a. I'm going to go to the store.
b. She's going to come tomorrow.
c. We're going to leave today.
d. They're going to eat at six.
e. He's going to be a teacher.

Optional Exercises and Activities – Student B

Unit 9

3. Student B: Ask Student A if the statements about Carol are true.

Example:
Did Carol live in Chicago in 1992?

a. Carol lived in Chicago in 1992.

b. She was a waitress.

c. She had a brother named Mark.

d. Mark and Carol often went to the beach.

e. Mark was an excellent swimmer.

f. She saved a young girl's life.

Now look at the information in the box and answer Student A's questions about Dave.

> **Information Box**
>
> g. Dave was a student in 1990.
>
> h. He studied accounting at UCLA.
>
> i. He was an excellent student.
>
> j. He graduated in 1992.
>
> k. He got a great job.
>
> l. He is still single.

Unit 16

2. Student B: Look at this map of New York City. You are at the corner of First Avenue and 37th Street. Ask Student A how to get to:
a. Radio City Music Hall
b. New York Public Library
c. Waldorf–Astoria Hotel

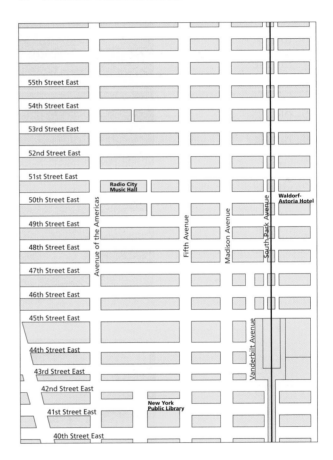

Wordfinder

Animals

1. bat
2. cat
3. crocodile
4. dog
5. elephant
6. lizard
7. mouse
8. parrot
9. pig
10. rabbit
11. snake
12. spider
13. tiger
14. wolf

Personal Description

Body type
1. tall
2. short
3. thin
4. fat

Eyes
5. small
6. big

Hair
7. long
8. short
9. curly
10. straight
11. blonde
12. brunette
13. redhead

General
14. great-looking
15. handsome
16. athletic

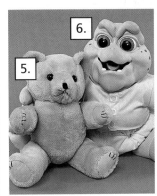
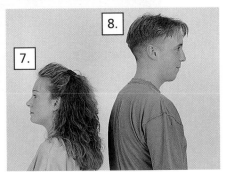

Transportation

1. airplane
2. balloon
3. bicycle
4. boat
5. bus
6. car
7. helicopter
8. motorcycle
9. pick-up
10. skis
11. skateboard
12. subway
13. taxi
14. train
15. truck

Parts of the Body

1. arm
2. chest
3. ear
4. eye
5. finger
6. foot
7. hand
8. head
9. knee
10. leg
11. mouth
12. neck
13. nose
14. stomach
15. toe

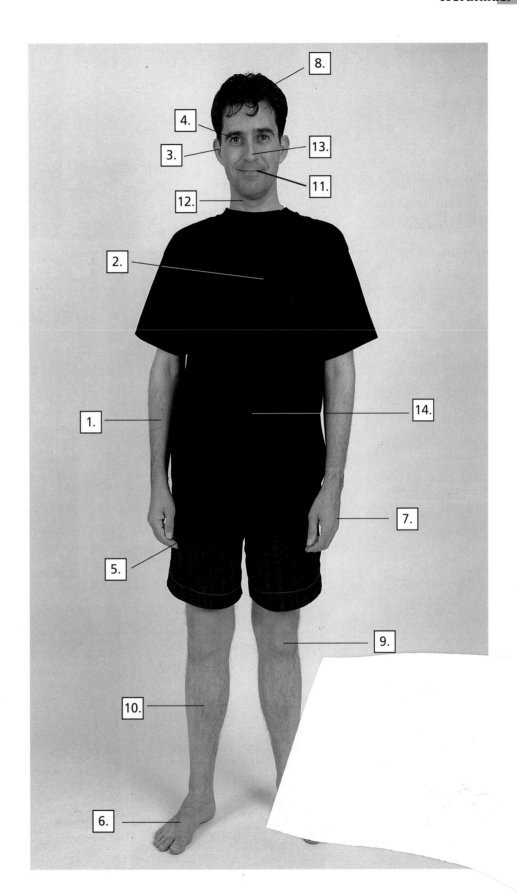

Geography

1. desert
2. forest
3. hills
4. lake
5. mountains
6. ocean
7. rain forest
8. river

Sports

1. baseball
2. basketball
3. bowling
4. boxing
5. diving
6. football
7. golf
8. hockey
9. sky-diving
10. soccer
11. swimming
12. tennis
13. track and field
14. volleyball

Feelings

1. angry
2. bored
3. confused
4. dizzy
5. excited
6. frightened
7. frustrated
8. happy
9. hungry
10. thirsty
11. worried

Clothes

1. blouse
2. dress
3. jeans
4. pants
5. shirt
6. shoes
7. skirt
8. socks
9. sweater
10. swimsuit
11. tennis shoes
12. tie
13. t-shirt

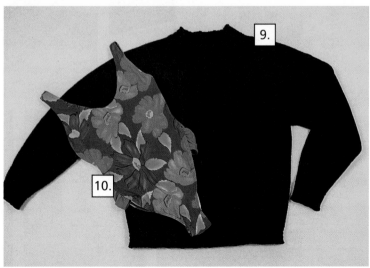

Household Chores

1. cut the grass/ mow the lawn
2. do/wash the dishes
3. dry the dishes
4. dust
5. feed the fish
6. fold
7. hang up the clothes
8. iron
9. make your bed
10. scrub
11. sweep
12. take out the garbage
13. vacuum
14. water the plants

Answer Key

Unit 2 – At the Start

The animals are a black widow spider, a gila monster, a wolf, a fruit bat and a garter snake.

a. The gila monster (a type of lizard), the wolf and the black widow spider are dangerous.
b. Some people in Mexico eat gila monsters.
c. Yes, the female black widow spider eats the male.
d. There aren't any snakes in Hawaii or Ireland.

Unit 6 – At the Start

1. They were from North America.
2. He was a famous movie actor in the 1920s.
3. The Supremes were a singing group in the 1960s.
4. Neil Armstrong.
5. Sputnik was the first spacecraft.
6. There were seven dwarfs.
7. He was a hero of Indian independence.
8. They were Christopher Columbus' three ships.
9. There were three Star Wars movies.
10. It was in Babylonia, which is now Iraq.

> ### Score
> **9–10** Wow! Super!!
> **7–8** Good going!
> **5–6** Pretty good.
> **0–4** You don't have a very good memory for trivia!

Unit 11 – At the Start

2. The niece was the killer.

Unit 12 – Practice

2. Ferdinand Magellan

Unit 18 – Reading

a. happy
b. disgusted
c. surprised
d. OK
e. excellent (Brazil)
f. beautiful (Brazil)
g. sad, bored
h. patient
i. shame

Unit 19 – At the Start

1. false
2. true
3. false
4. true
5. true

Irregular verbs

Infinitive	Past	Infinitive	Past	Infinitive	Past
to be	was/were	to give	gave	to see	saw
to beat	beat	to go	went	to sell	sold
to begin	began	to grow	grew	to send	sent
to bite	bit	to have	had	to shut	shut
to break	broke	to hear	heard	to sing	sang
to bring	brought	to hide	hid	to sink	sank
to build	built	to hold	held	to sit	sat
to burn	burned/burnt	to hurt	hurt	to sleep	slept
to buy	bought	to keep	kept	to speak	spoke
to catch	caught	to kneel	knelt	to spend	spent
to choose	chose	to know	knew	to spill	spilled/spilt
to come	came	to lay	laid	to stand	stood
to cost	cost	to leave	left	to steal	stole
to cut	cut	to lend	lent	to sweep	swept
to dive	dove	to let	let	to swim	swam
to do	did	to lie	lay	to take	took
to draw	drew	to lose	lost	to teach	taught
to drink	drank	to make	made	to tear	tore
to drive	drove	to mean	meant	to tell	told
to eat	ate	to meet	met	to think	thought
to fall	fell	to pay	paid	to throw	threw
to feel	felt	to put	put	to understand	understood
to fight	fought	to read	read	to wake	woke
to find	found	to ride	rode	to wear	wore
to fly	flew	to ring	rang	to win	won
to forget	forgot	to rise	rose	to write	wrote
to freeze	froze	to run	ran		
to get	got	to say	said		